THE
MICHAELMAS
DAISY

Paul Marriner

Bluescale Publishing

www.bluescalepublishing.co.uk

Cover design by by JD Smith Design Ltd, www.jdsmith-design.co.uk.

Bluescale Publishing

ISBN 978-1-9996200-8-0 (ebook)

ISBN 978-1-9996200-7-3 (paperback)

Dedication

For those in need of care – you matter and are deserving;
we can learn much from you, especially about ourselves

For those with the compassion, patience, wisdom and true
humanity to provide care – you are special and have much
to teach us

To all: You are allowed to live with hope

To Florence: Thank you

Author's Note

There are many reasons people need support and care; dementia is but one, and there are many variations of dementia. Each person requiring care will have unique personal circumstances and challenges, as will their carers. This novel is not an attempt to write of typical, usual, common or expected circumstances – if those things even exist. Nor is it intended to act as some kind of guide for carers, either practically or emotionally. But if you are a carer or someone in need of care, it is written in your honour, and as a reminder that you are valued, not alone, and allowed to find room for laughter and hope in your lives, hard as that can often be.

THE
MICHAELMAS
DAISY

Chapter 1
Beverley Cooper

My name is Beverley Cooper. I am dead.

I watch over them. I am heartbroken.

The Michaelmas Daisy

Chapter 2
Monday 6th May
Tiddlywink Old Man

The day before I died, I whispered to Philippa that I would watch over them. And I do. But, of course, I'd meant I would keep them safe and help them to be happy. I can't. I can only watch over them. It breaks my heart.

Philippa Cooper is my daughter. Today is Monday, 6th May, 2019. Bin day. Philippa is in Kenny's bedroom. Kenny is her father, my widower husband. He's still in bed, at just gone ten. I've never got used to that. He'd spent his working life on the railways, usually up and out of the house by six thirty. And when first retired, he'd still be up by seven, bringing me tea in bed whether I was awake or not. But these days he stays under the covers until Philippa coaxes him out. The bed is a fancy hospital contraption. With the 'head' end raised, he can see out of the bay window. He asks Philippa who the people are in yellow jackets at the top of his drive. Electric motors whir as she presses the button to raise the bed a little higher, then holds back the net curtains so he can see properly.

'Bin men, Dad. It's Monday.'

'Well tell 'em to be bin and gone,' Kenny says, without laughing. Philippa laughs even though she has heard this joke every Monday for the last three years. On hearing Philippa laugh, so does he, pleased to have been funny.

Philippa makes sure the bed's guard rail is securely in place, 'Just going to bring the wheelies in, Dad,' and nips out to the front to return the green and blue bins back to their rightful place, just in front of the garage doors that never open.

'Don't be long,' Kenny shouts to her back.

It's a bright, cloudless morning. The sort of morning

that, fifty years ago or more, was perfect for taking Philippa down to the park. The roundabouts and swings were a welcome diversion and I wasted many hours watching her play. No, not wasted: enjoyed; was nurtured by; felt my heart swell; learnt about myself; planned a future, lived a present; promised I would be the best wife and mother. And here I am, still watching, still making promises.

'Morning, Joyce,' Philippa calls across the fence to our neighbour.

'Morning, Philippa,' Joyce calls back. 'How's Kenny?'

I am the only one who calls him Kenny. Joyce is over-familiar to call him that, but then she's been a good neighbour for many years.

'Good spirits, thanks. Not as nimble on his feet as he used to be, but then he is eighty-nine,' replies Philippa.

Philippa: master of understatement.

'Hope I make it to that age,' Joyce says. They both laugh.

She might not say that if she'd seen Kenny lately. She was born just eight years after him. How is it he's decades older than her?

'How's Shogun?' Philippa asks. She always does. A useful question to deflect attention.

'Pain in the wotsit. Sorry 'bout all the barking.'

'No problem. We don't mind. Anytime you need us to look after him just say. Dad likes having Shogun around. He still misses Blofeld.'

Blofeld died in the early 90s. Stupid name for a dog, especially as she was a bitch, but Kenny loved – loves – Bond films. Of course Connery was – is – his favourite. I had a soft spot for Lazenby.

Joyce says something but it's lost under the noise of wheelie bins being dragged back to their regimented places. Philippa smiles an acknowledgement and finishes the chat with encouragement to, 'Have a good day.'

There was a time, when she left the house for school, I'd say, 'Have a good day. Get what you can from it. It won't

4

come round again.' I can't remember the last time I heard her say that to anyone. Perhaps she never has. She didn't have children. I suspect that was Ciaran's fault – and who'd have thought that, what with him being a Catholic and all. Mind you, I'm not one to talk, Philippa's an only child, sort of. Not for want of trying.

Joyce next door has a son, Lewis. I think he's two years younger than Philippa, maybe fifty-six. A shy man as I remember, but well-mannered with kind blue eyes. I wonder what happened to him, where he now lives. Philippa never asks Joyce about him. Shame. He might be single, or divorced, like Philippa.

'Only me, Dad!' Philippa calls as she comes back into the bedroom.

'Where have you been?'

'Putting the bins back,' Philippa says patiently. 'Time to get up.'

'In a minute.'

'Breakfast awaits,' Philippa says, sweeping an arm theatrically towards the hall.

This is a fib. She won't start breakfast until Kenny's personal care is finished and he's dressed.

Personal care. What a polite phrase for such an undignified exercise, but Philippa just gets on with it.

In some ways I'm glad I went before I had to clean and change a grown man. By his mid-seventies I'd pretty much stopped touching his 'bits' and, to be honest, they're even less appealing now, haha. But I have a pleasing memory of the first time Kenny pawed at me – 1953, round the back of The Half-Way House, walking me home. I say 'paw' as if that was a bad thing, it wasn't. I was 'pawing' back. We were like exploring octopuses, and I didn't mind a bit of roughness, it showed he was keen. Actually, make that clumsiness. Kenny was never a violent man, so when he got carried away like that, well, I knew it was 'cos he was proper keen, and who doesn't want that? And, though he was a bit clumsy that night, he grew to be careful. I think he was worried that with him being close to six foot and me just five foot three, he might hurt me. He never did. I think I'm blushing. I didn't know I still could.

'Please, Dad, time to get up.' Philippa is pushing the hoist into place by the bed. The hoist is awkward and heavy.

'In a minute.'

'C'mon. Time to be a bobby-dazzler.'

'In a minute,' Kenny repeats.

'Tiddlywink old man, suck a …' Philippa starts to sing.

'… lemon if you can …' Kenny picks it up.

'… if you can't …' Philippa prompts as she edges the hoist into place.

'… suck a lemon, suck an old tin can.' And by the time the verse is finished Kenny is pushing himself, slowly, oh so slowly, oh so very slowly, and with difficulty, up to sitting. Philippa lowers the bed guard and pulls on a pair of blue disposable surgical gloves, explaining what she's doing at each step; always. She helps Kenny spin, slowly, oh so slowly, to drop his legs over the side, and lowers the mattress to the right height so his feet are just off the floor. She asks him to rest his feet on the hoist's footplates and Kenny tries, he really tries, but he can't move his feet the necessary few inches. It's not that he's in pain, but it's painful to watch. So much effort. So little result. And every day it surprises him. It's not as though he's had a stroke or accident or anything, but so much of his body simply no longer obeys. Philippa moves his feet for him. They look a little bloated, pale and yet pink at the same time. She slips a sling around his back, clicks the front clasp, and runs the straps under his arms. There is fear in Kenny eyes. He has done this – had this done to him – a hundred times, yet it's always the first and there is fear. But he trusts, and reaches up to hold the handles as politely suggested by Philippa. The sling is hooked to the hoist and Philippa uses the remote control to take up the slack. At the point of tension, where the machine starts to raise Kenny, there is a momentary pause then a small jolt, no matter how smooth Philippa tries to make the transition, and it's this jolt, every time, that makes Kenny grab a sudden breath, every time. It's a gasp of surprise but sounds like a short, sharp cry of pain. Kenny looks at Philippa as the hoist slowly rises and, not wanting to appear frightened, gives a false smile to show he can be brave. He is so, so brave and my heart breaks for the day's first time, again. He joins Philippa chanting,

'Tiddlywink old man
Suck a lemon if you can
If you can't suck a lemon
Suck an old tin can.'

I don't remember when Kenny started singing this ditty. I wonder where it came from. Perhaps I'd gone before he learnt it, though, of course, I haven't gone far. I'm still here, watching – oh, and in the small but expensive wooden casket on the sideboard; nice bit of mahogany, chosen by Philippa. Kenny just … couldn't. For a while, my casket was tucked away on a shelf in the conservatory next to a yucca plant that Kenny brought home when he retired, years ago. Lord knows why they thought he'd want a yucca, but they also gave him a set of luggage. It would be a lie to say we got proper use from it.

Philippa brought both the yucca and my ashes in to the lounge when she moved in to look after Kenny. The yucca died soon after. My ashes live on.

Philippa shuffles the hoist through ninety degrees. Kenny's weight is taken by the sling around his back and under his arms. His feet are on the hoist's footplate but bear little, if any, weight. The hoist is heavy, with small wheels suited to a hard floor, making it difficult to move on the carpet. But then the Social Services lady did say it's usually a two-man job. Philippa has to use all her own weight to jiggle it into the right position. She pulls down Kenny's pyjama trousers and checks the contents of the incontinence pants. They will be wet, of course, but hopefully not double-soiled. By the lack of smell, Philippa guesses not. She's right. That's four days in a row she has guessed right – a record – though to be honest when he's double-soiled even I can smell it. Philippa tears the perforated seams apart on both sides and removes the damp pants from between Kenny's legs. The seams don't tear easily but Philippa is strong. She always was bigger than her friends, but gentle and easy-going. It meant she was a disappointment to the school netball teacher. I was proud of that. But it wasn't easy for her, a gawky teenager, and she didn't believe me when I told her one day her friends would kill – better than dying, I can vouch – for legs as long as hers. She folds Kenny's pants neatly in on themselves and puts them in a small biodegradable bin-bag. She does all this quickly, practiced. Kenny's becoming agitated. She soaks and squeezes out the flannel from the bowl of warm soapy water on the dressing table. The hoist won't fit in the bathroom and it's difficult to wash him thoroughly when he's sitting on the commode, so she quickly washes Kenny 'down there', front and back while he 'dangles'. She dries him off and positions the wheeled commode chair so she can lower him onto it. Kenny, predictably, draws a sharp intake of breath as his bare bottom touches cold plastic.

'We need to invent a heated toilet seat,' Philippa says, every morning.

'I should coco,' says Kenny, every morning.

Philippa inspects and smells the bed to see if the pants leaked; if the sheets need washing. They were washed yesterday but don't need it today. Good. That's time saved. She pushes Kenny on the commode, out of the bedroom, down the hall, through the kitchen, and into the bathroom she had put in the extension, cautioning, 'Try to keep your feet off the floor, Dad.' She should attach footrests but they are awkward to fix and catch too easily on the door frames.

I don't go into the bathroom. They don't need me to

check the ablutions – fancy word; Philippa would laugh – are satisfactory. This is where she strip washes him all over as best she can while he is sitting on the commode. I made it a point long ago never to go into the bathroom when either Kenny or Philippa were there. They deserve some privacy. At night I never join Philippa when she's sleeping. I stay with Kenny. When I see he's dreaming, I like to think I'm there too.

The nights are long.

The bathroom door closes behind them and I hear a long, wet fart.

'Was that you or me?' asks Kenny. Does he not know or is he teasing?

Philippa laughs, 'Wherever you may be …' she begins,

'… let your wind go free,' sings Kenny.

As I say, perhaps it's as well I went first.

The Michaelmas Daisy

Chapter 3
Friday 10th May
A Spoonful Of Sugar

It's nearly eleven. Breakfast at this time isn't unusual. I don't know exactly what goes on in the bathroom, but it takes a long time, and, when they emerge, Kenny has been washed – 'top' and 'tail', especially 'tail' – and shaved – 'top' but not 'tail', haha. His teeth are in, hair, what there is, combed, and spectacles in place, albeit smeared. It irritates me when his spectacles are greasy. I wish I could clean them. He's wheeled back through the kitchen and hall to the bedroom. The hoist is used again so Philippa can dress him in new incontinence pants and clean trousers before transferring him to the indoor wheelchair to finish. Strong as Philippa is, it's difficult to pull him forward in the chair with one arm, while slipping on vest, shirt and jumper with the other. Kenny used to be nearly six foot but though he's shorter now, and there's simply less of him, everywhere, it's still a two-person job. So many things are. Finally, socks and slippers go on and Kenny is pushed back down the hall to the kitchen, Philippa reminding him to lift his feet so they don't drag on the floor, though it makes no difference. Philippa then returns to the bedroom to wash the commode's seat and retrieve the bowl of warm water used to give him that first wash 'down there'. As she leaves the bedroom, Philippa squirts a dab of antiseptic gel into her hands, rubs them gently and looks back to the bed. It needs to be changed today, third time since Monday, despite the bigger plastic sheet she bought from Amazon. That's a lot of washing. That's a lot of bed making. That's a lot of backache. It's another two-person job. I am here. I am of no use.

Today, Kenny seems quite content and is muttering quietly. Philippa doesn't catch it but doesn't ask him to repeat, not like she used to. In the kitchen, she puts Kenny's favourite – make that habitual – cereal in a bowl with

11

chopped banana, blueberries and honey. He has semi-skimmed milk, better for his cholesterol, as if that matters any more. Kenny can just about manage to feed himself while Philippa prepares five tablets and a glass of orange juice. No wonder it's nearly half eleven now. Philippa finally sits. Her breakfast was three hours ago, so she sips black coffee, ignoring the TV, then jumps at the doorbell.

I hate the harsh front doorbell. We moved to this house in autumn 1984, getting on thirty-five years ago, and Kenny said his first job would be to change that, 'Bloody cheap clanger.' I'd suggested it wasn't the number one priority – getting the boiler running, replacing the light fittings taken by the tight-fisted previous owners, and fixing the fence so Blofeld wouldn't escape were more important. Kenny didn't agree with me and we had an argument. Our first. Not first argument, just first in this house. I won. The dog needed to be let out into the back garden to do her business and promptly squeezed through the broken fence into next door. That's a Jack Russell for you. Still, at least it was an excuse to go and introduce ourselves to the neighbours. Smiling faces were needed for the neighbours, naturally, but afterwards we both stewed over the petty row about the fence.

Later that evening, while I was watching *Coronation Street*, Kenny slipped out to the garden, picked a Michaelmas daisy and presented it to me on one knee,

> 'The Michaelmas daisy grows so tall
> It sees right over the garden wall,
> I wonder, I wonder what it can see
> For the Michaelmas daisy is taller than me ...'

... and pecked me on the cheek.

'Is this for being wrong about the fence?' I asked, sniffing the small purple flower, and laughing at the silly rhyme.

'No, it's to finish the argument. Doesn't matter who's

wrong or right.'

And, of course, he was right about that.

Our painfully harsh doorbell has never been replaced. Thirty-five years and we never got round to it.

So Philippa jumps at the penetrating two-tone, tuneless chime. Kenny looks up calmly from his bowl of cereal. His hearing is poor. 'Was that the door? Who is it?' he asks Philippa's back as she walks down the hall.

'We didn't expect anyone, did we, Dad?' Philippa shows a nurse through. I was going to say *the* nurse, but, as it's a different one every time, not quite true. He's come to take blood. Philippa asks who made the arrangements and why.

'I don't know. I just got the job on the system,' he says.

Philippa watches as the nurse puts on a smile and introduces himself to Kenny, talking slowly and loudly. I shout, 'He's unwell, not stupid!' They don't notice me. No one does anymore. I miss that. I heard some woman on the TV complain that once she turned fifty it was as if she'd become invisible. Ha, she should try being dead.

The nurse, I already forget his name, rolls up Kenny's shirtsleeve. Philippa turns down the TV. Kenny pays little attention to either. A small piece of banana has fallen from his spoon, and the pale, dull yellow stands out against the bright blue plastic table cloth. Kenny picks up the banana remnant for inspection while the nurse rubs and taps the crook of his other elbow, looking for a vein. Kenny pays no heed as a cold wipe disinfects the area and an elastic band is pulled tight around his withered bicep. He doesn't flinch when the needle pierces crimplene skin. He never was afraid of needles. He never was squeamish. I learnt that the first time I met him, outside the Ace Café on the North Circular.

I'd gone there in the sidecar of my second boyfriend's BSA. While we were drinking coffee and arguing over Nat

King Cole or Johnnie Ray for best singer – I was always for Cole – there was an ear-splitting roar of engine, the smashing of glass, grinding of metal, and an explosion of bursting tyre, all in an explosive second. Then sudden silence. The café was shocked into inaction before everyone pushed outside to find a mangled wreckage of three or four bikes and a single rider crumpled on his side, bleeding heavily from a lot of places it seemed. The smell of petrol was strong but didn't stop smokers from edging forward. My date rushed ... to check his own bike was ok. I was spellbound by the slowly growing pool of blood next to a similar pool of oil. They merged, but didn't mix, into a psychedelic swirl, reflecting the lights from the café. Kenny – I didn't know his name at the time – pushed his way through the crowd, to the injured biker, calling for tea towels, flannels and bungee cords. He gently turned the biker onto his back. Unlike many riders, he wore a helmet, but, when someone went to remove it, Kenny told him not to be so, 'Bloody stupid.' Under the fluorescent light shining through the café's glass, I saw the wide rip in the leather jacket, and the deep, ragged gash underneath, oozing blood. I was mesmerised rather than sickened. Kenny pulled off his t-shirt – he was tall and well-built – and stuffed it into the wound, calmly asking where the towels were and had anyone rung the ambulance.

It was an hour before the mess had been cleaned up – bikes and person. Kenny stood off to one side, holding his blood-soaked t-shirt, shivering in the growing cold, smoking a king-sized cigarette – posh. I offered him my cardigan and he laughed warmly, but declined, saying he wouldn't want to stain or stretch it. I asked behind the café counter if they had a lost property box and found a blue, light woollen man's jumper he could have. When I asked if he was a doctor he laughed again and explained he'd worked alongside army nurses during National Service. I said it was lucky a person with training had been here. He made a joke about being an expert in scraping shit, cleaning pus and mopping up blood and guts without puking, that's all. He made it funny. I asked his name and he asked mine. I told him, 'Beverley,' and he asked if I had two sisters. It took me a couple of seconds to get it, but that was funny too.

I went home on the back of his Triumph Thunderbird. It didn't have a sidecar but what the hell, I was wearing slacks.

We didn't snog until that third date, round the back of The Half-Way House. What kind of girl do you think I am – was?

'Tea or coffee?' Philippa asks the nurse.

'No thanks.' The nurse doesn't look up from the laptop on which he types heavily with two fingers. His uniform makes him look older than he probably is. I'd guess mid-forties, and carrying it well. His features are set firm but there are plenty of laughter lines at his eyes. If only Philippa can get him to smile.

'Are you sure? It's no problem.' She speaks so well, so clearly. Kenny always said she gets that from me. I got it from my mum who was determined I shouldn't be lumped in with the kids from the other end of the street, down by the bathworks. I'm not sure speaking well helped much, but she did teach me a lot of clever words the others didn't know, and it did impress Kenny – at the beginning, at least – so the effort was worth it. He stopped swearing soon after we started going out, and he tried hard to speak nicely around Mum and Dad, especially Mum.

The nurse doesn't answer.

'Many calls to make today?' Philippa asks, and I know she's being more than just polite. Some conversation, any conversation, would be welcome.

The nurse nods.

'My husband was a district nurse, for a while,' Philippa offers. At this, the nurse fakes a smile, which doesn't add to those laughter lines, and packs away his equipment. Philippa sees him to the door, with thanks for coming.

'He was in a hurry,' Philippa says to Kenny, putting her half-finished coffee in the microwave for reheating.

Kenny ignores her. He alternates between inspecting the piece of banana and finishing breakfast, slowly. Philippa watches television, or, rather, stares at the screen. She mutters, 'Hard work, nursing.'

Ciaran, her ex, was a nurse. Perhaps he still is. It was unusual for a man back in the day. Shame he's no longer around. Kenny liked him – so did I – and I expect he'd have been a good carer, though who's to say he'd have wanted to be? Wiping your father-in-law's bottom isn't in the marriage vows, though I suppose it might be covered by 'for worse'.

As far as I know, Philippa hasn't been out with a man since the divorce. Eight years. Shame. She's a good-looking woman – fifty-eight, full head of greying hair, tall, thanks to those long legs, even if they do carry a little more weight these days. But she kept her figure, a little thicker in the waist, but curvy as ever, perhaps more so in places – not having children helped. And she's smart, dresses well – at least when she goes up the shops, though more and more these days she has it all delivered. She's not going to meet anyone that way. I wonder what would happen if Ciaran, the nurse, turned up one day. There's a joke there about, 'Already having the house and car, and now wanting blood,' which Philippa could make funny – she has a way with words. I can imagine Ciaran laughing. He laughed a lot. They laughed a lot, at first. He was laughing the first time I met him.

I took – take – pride in being the one that brought them together. It was my idea for Philippa to join the art class at the community centre. She'd left school at sixteen for an apprenticeship as a draughtsman – woman? person? The world is moving on and it's not that I don't want to move with it, I just don't know how, which I suppose is not a surprise. Anyway, Philippa was bold to train as a draughtsperson.

It was hard for Philippa in those days – an engineering company on an industrial estate, flaking art deco facades trying to flatter cold, corrugated iron roof workshops, naked neon strip lights, dirty windows, the smell of oil and metal, the smell of men – haha – so sure of themselves as to be patronising, men so unsure of themselves as to be condescending, casual contempt, plotted bullying.

It was a small firm, making instruments for airplanes. Kenny and I were proud of her and she must have been a good draughtsperson – they kept her on for thirty-eight years, an entire career in one company. She must have been, still is, smart, determined and strong. The other women on site were either in the canteen or typing pool, but that didn't stop her making friends with them.

Are draughtspersons usually good at drawing and painting? Philippa is. She always was, and joined the local art group in her late teens. On the first night she went, as she readied to leave, I remember Kenny teasing.

'Let me know when it's paint-a-nude night. I might join.'

'No one wants to paint a flabby old man, Dad,' said Philippa.

'I meant to draw, not model,' said Kenny.

'I know.' Philippa laughed.

'Although, I once did a bit of modelling,' said Kenny. 'Cardigans in a catalogue. Still could.'

'Of course, dear,' I'd said and it was true, just after he left the army, but before I met him.

By the time Philippa went to art class, Kenny was in his mid-forties but still strong and straight-backed. Our back garden needed a lot of maintenance. Oh, and he still looked a bit like Lazenby.

Philippa had come back from the class in good spirits, very good spirits. It was a day or two until she mentioned, casually, she'd met Ciaran at the class, a trainee nurse a couple of years older than her.

'And did he model in the nuddy?' Kenny teased.

'Not yet, Dad,' she said as she left us in the lounge, speechless.

Happy days.

After divorcing Ciaran she went back to the art classes. She even ran them for a while after moving back here to look after her dad.

I hope that nurse comes back. He was acceptably handsome, if a bit young. Not that there needs to be any romance, just a chat would be nice.

Kenny has finished the cereal and fruit. Philippa tells him he has done well and moves the glass of orange juice closer on the table saying, 'Tablets.' She removes the bowl and lines the pills on the placemat in front of Kenny. They are not quite straight.

'What are they for?' Kenny asks as he nudges the blue and white pill to be exactly in line.

Philippa smiles. 'They keep you alive, Dad.'

Kenny looks over the top of his spectacles. 'Well that's a bloody waste then.' His eyes are red and dull. He doesn't pick up the glass of juice.

'C'mon, Dad. What would Mum say? You need to take your tablets. We don't want Mum to be cross.' I follow Philippa's gaze to the picture next to the toaster, and look at myself. I'm not even thirty in the photo, sitting on a beach somewhere, laughing at something long forgotten. I was pretty, petite and funny. I like to think I still am. It was only those last few months I wasn't – or was it the last couple of years? God, I hope not.

'Where's Mum?' Kenny looks to Philippa.

'She's gone, Dad.'

I force a smile, trying to match my picture.

'Oh. What's this for?' Kenny picks up a small yellow capsule.

'Ah, that's the one that makes your jokes funny.' Philippa tries. Kenny, of course, doesn't understand the attempt at humour. 'It's for your blood pressure.' Philippa feels obliged to explain, as if that makes any more sense to Kenny, who shrugs and says,

'I don't want it,' to close the conversation, and gives the tablet to Philippa, who starts to sing,

'Just a spoonful of ...' then waits to hear.

'... sugar, makes the ...' sings Kenny, but doesn't finish. He's distracted. A solitary blueberry lies in his lap, an escapee from his breakfast bowl. He picks it from his trousers, studies, then crushes it. Juice spurts onto his fingers. He tugs at a pocket for a handkerchief but Philippa is quicker with a tissue and wipes his hand while slipping the tablet into Kenny's mouth, singing,

'... makes the tablet go down.'

Kenny sips juice and swallows. It takes another minute before all the tablets are gone. Philippa wipes his mouth and chin, and they sit in silence for a while. Then Kenny looks over to Philippa, points at her, smiles, and starts, 'Tinker, tailor, soldier, sailor, rich man, poor man, beggarman, thief,' waving his finger vaguely between the two of them as he speaks, and somehow finishing up pointing at Philippa, and laughs.

'You're a naughty man,' says Philippa, laughing with him.

The Michaelmas Daisy

Chapter 4
Saturday 25th May
Holding The Rails

We're watching a film about the 1966 World Cup; still at the breakfast table: Kenny; Philippa; me – sort of. It's getting on for twelve. Every day takes a little longer. I've never been a football follower, let alone a fan, but this match was a happy time, a captured time, a time both frozen and burning bright in my memory, and, surely, hopefully, Kenny's and Philippa's. July 1966. A time, I pray, for which we truly share the same memory. Does Kenny, still? Though it may not come easily to his mind, I'm convinced it's there.

'That goal's coming up soon, Dad. Will it cross the line? What d'you think?' asks Philippa.

Kenny isn't paying attention. He's watching a chaffinch pick at the bird feeder hanging outside the kitchen window. This is a disappointment to Philippa and I want to tell her that I'm watching the match. I remember. I was there. I am here. It's been nearly eight years since I died and still I can't bear it – not the death, the watching – and yet what else am I to do?

I shout, 'Goal!' as the ball cannons off the crossbar, into the ground, behind the line; of course. The Russian linesman raises his flag.

It was the first game Philippa watched all the way through, even – especially – extra time. She was nearly six, and no football fan, but even she understood it was important. The shops were empty, the streets quiet, the living rooms stocked with cans of pale ale, pots of tea and Battenburg cake – ironic as England were playing West Germany. We even had a wooden rattle – that was fun, the first couple of times. Philippa didn't understand the game and Kenny didn't explain. It wasn't necessary. The drama was more important and exciting than the sport. Philippa felt it. And afterwards she was out in the garden, kicking a tennis ball against the conservatory, close to the French doors, but that didn't matter, not today. Kenny didn't shout at her to be careful, he joined her, then called me out, and in the late afternoon July sun, the three of us won the World Cup all over again.

I may be dead but I can taste the salt of my tears, both that day and now.

'You're missing it, Dad.' Philippa tries to catch Kenny's attention. 'This is the last time we'll be able to see it for a while. We're stopping the subscription next month. Freeview only from then.'

This means nothing to Kenny. It doesn't mean much to me, except I've heard Philippa on the phone to Sky, cancelling the monthly sub. Though there is Kenny's state pension, his railway pension, Attendance Allowance, Philippa's work pension, and her Carer's Allowance, times are still hard. The water, council tax, gas and 'leccy bills are frightening and Philippa's still running her car. Not to mention this new phone-broadband thing she had put in. And incontinence pads would be cheaper than the pants, but Philippa will give Kenny as much dignity as she can. So money is tight. I know they are dipping into Kenny and Philippa's savings. I tell Philippa not to worry, we have known hard times. Something always turned up. Back in the day, when I had to, I'd clean toilets, deliver leaflets, serve on the fish stall – not for long, too smelly –sew dresses – I wasn't very good – assemble Christmas crackers at home by the thousand – for pennies – be a dinner lady, serve in the baker's shop, solder circuit boards – I had a steady hand – pack cigarettes; anything to bring in a few bob when the coal bill was higher than expected, or the rates were due, or I'd miscalculated a Kays catalogue payment. We never doubted we'd get by. Kenny and Philippa will too. I tell her. Sometimes, when I say such things, she looks over to my photo by the toaster and I wonder … does she hear? I wonder. I pray. I doubt it, though I'm sure she knows it's what I would say, which is as good as being there, right?

There's a knock at the door. Philippa disconnected that painful bell a couple of days ago, finally. I miss it already.

'That'll be Shogun. Stay there,' Philippa tells Kenny, and I laugh – like he's going anywhere. He's busy folding and re-folding a napkin into a perfect square. It takes great concentration and is calming, for both of us.

Philippa opens the door and Joyce presents Shogun into the opening gap. She holds him like a baby with a soiled nappy and the dog does not look impressed. He's a bright white West Highland Terrier with an ego ten times his size. He checks out Philippa for a couple of seconds before recognising her and wriggles to be put down. Joyce tells Shogun, not Philippa, that Lewis – her son – will pick him up about four, but Shogun is already down the hall, desperate to see Kenny. Kenny will be thrilled to see Shogun. I go back to the kitchen while Joyce hands over Shogun's lead, lunch and treats. I can't bear to listen while she patronisingly explains, again, when Shogun needs to eat, when he needs to be let out, when he … blah, blah, blah. Philippa has mastered 24/7 care and attention for a grown, immobile, incontinent, vascular dementia-suffering man, and Joyce thinks she can't handle a small dog? But Philippa smiles and nods.

I laugh to myself – of course, who else would hear? – as Kenny breaks off a piece of jam smothered toast and holds it for Shogun. The dog jumps up, forelegs on the wheels of Kenny's chair, and all but takes off Kenny's fingers, biting at the sweet treat. Kenny giggles as Shogun drops it on the floor, and chases the piece of food round the kitchen, licking off the jam and butter, leaving the toast.

Philippa pretends to be cross. She'll have to clear up the mess.

Having licked the toast clean, Shogun explores downstairs, then upstairs, checking to ensure nothing has changed, then another quick round downstairs before waiting by the back door. Philippa lets him out – those fences were fixed long ago – and watches him through the kitchen window for a half a minute. 'Tell you what, Dad,' she calls over her shoulder, 'if the weather stays dry we'll take Shogun for a walk later.'

This is no small ambition. Better start getting ready now.

Kenny doesn't hear. Or he does. I don't know, and suspect his, 'Eh?' response is more an automatic reaction than an acknowledgement he didn't catch it.

Philippa takes a deep breath and repeats the suggestion.

'What's a shogun?' Kenny asks.

Philippa is about to explain when there is another knock on the door. She checks her watch. 'They're early.'

'Who are?' Kenny doesn't look away from the TV – the match has finally caught his attention as Bobby Moore lifts the trophy. 'Is he still going?'

'Who?'

'Him.' Kenny points at the TV.

'No, Dad. And it's probably the Occupational Therapist at the door. They want to see how you're getting on.'

'Tell 'em we don't want any.'

'Of course, Dad.'

'Kenny Cooper?' asks the burly man at the door.

Does my daughter look like an eighty-nine-year-old man? Where the bloody hell do they get these people? One advantage of being dead is I can use the word 'bloody' as often as I like. In life I'd only said it twice. The first was outside the infants' school when I caught some snotty kid bullying Philippa and, when I told him off, his stuck-up mother told me to mind my own business. I quietly suggested she better keep her ugly, miserable kid away from my Philippa if she bloody knew what was good for her. I'm not sure I used the 'B' word in quite the right place, but it worked. After that, Philippa never had any trouble from other kids and the other mums were wary of me, which I didn't mind. The second was years later. We were in our forties. Kenny and I had a weekend in Weymouth – Philippa was on a school trip – and we went to see *Confessions Of A Window Cleaner*. I think we were both a bit embarrassed, I know I was, but it was naughty rather than 'porn', if not as funny as I'd hoped. Later, in our shabby guest house bedroom, after a couple of glasses of sherry from the bottle we sneaked in, Kenny kept hinting about the film and asked, awkwardly, if I'd ever 'talked dirty'. As I'd been a virgin until I'd met him, I wondered why he thought I might have. But after a day wandering Weymouth beach in the sun, in a, for me, skimpy summer dress, watching a naughty film, gulping a couple of sherries on an empty stomach, and wearing a new satin nightie, I was willing to try. So was Kenny, who was sensitive enough not to giggle when I whispered, 'I bloody well want you,' – which is even less sexy than it sounds. Anyway, we ended up laughing like drains, then had one of the best 'early nights' I can remember. I am blushing. Just as well Philippa can't see or hear me.

'Kenny Cooper?' the man at the door repeats.

'No, I'm Philippa, his daughter. Come through.' Ever patient Philippa.

The man doesn't answer.

'Dad, the man from Occupational Therapy is here. To see how you're doing.'

'Occupational Health,' says the man, 'not Therapy.'

'What's the difference?' Philippa asks and the man smiles patronisingly.

'I'm with Social Services, Special Services Team, Home Resources.'

'Not Occupational Therapy then?'

'No. They're with the NHS, the Specialist Home Resources and Services Team, though we do sometimes refer to them and get referrals from them.'

'Of course,' says Philippa. 'This is Kenny.'

'Cooper?'

Philippa rolls her eyes.

Kenny looks to Philippa and asks, 'What does he want?'

'Kenny Cooper?' The OH man asks again, looking down to the floor as he steps on the piece of toast Shogun didn't want. The OH man runs a quick glance round the kitchen, not yet tidied from breakfast. He asks Kenny, 'Do you know your date of birth?'

'Yes, do you?' says Kenny, passing to the man a half-eaten piece of toast. The OH – not OT – man feels obliged to take it and holds it for a few seconds, unsure what to do. Philippa takes it and offers a drink which is gratefully accepted. The OH man chats to Kenny while Philippa makes tea. Kenny relaxes as the man makes him laugh with a joke about racing round the garden.

'I was just about to move him into the lounge, onto the riser/recliner,' says Philippa as she passes the OH man a cup of tea, 'But I can do it later.'

'That's ok, there's no rush, I can wait, and I'd like to see how his mobility is.'

Mobility? If only. Philippa smiles awkwardly. I suspect she'd rather not have an audience watching her move Kenny.

'And perhaps I can help,' offers the OH man, stepping aside to watch – judge? – as Philippa takes the brakes off Kenny's wheelchair so she can move it away from the table. Then she removes the bib Kenny has been wearing. It's stained. Another one for the wash. She used to use disposable ones but they are more expensive. Philippa leaves it on the table with the rest of the debris from breakfast saying, 'Feet off the floor, Dad,' as she wheels the chair through to the lounge, careful not to catch Kenny's elbows on the door frames. Kenny begins to sing, 'Pack up all my …' then forgets the words so Philippa continues,

'Cares and woe, here I go …'

They sing together, 'Singing low, bye bye blackbird.'

'Is that a song from the old days?' OH man asks,

following the wheelchair into the room.

'No. Who are you?' Kenny asks kindly.

The OH man laughs.

Philippa leaves the wheelchair – brakes back on – close to the recliner/raiser and goes to the bedroom to drag in the hoist, trying to take it through the doors without chipping paintwork. With the hoist in front of the wheelchair she puts the sling around Kenny's back and under his arms.

'Five, four, three …' Philippa counts down – her best *Thunderbirds* impression.

'Two, one,' finishes Kenny and Philippa presses the button for the hoist to lift Kenny. As ever, at the point of tension, Kenny cries out in surprise, as if in pain. Philippa looks to the OH man but he doesn't react.

With Kenny in the air, feet lightly touching the hoist's footplates, Philippa unbrakes the wheelchair, moves it out of the way, and swivels the hoist round – difficult as it catches on the carpet – so that Kenny's now backing on to the lounge chair which is fully raised. The hoist lowers Kenny to the seat. Philippa helps Kenny lean forward so the sling can be unclicked and removed before an old pillow, with clean cover, is stuffed behind him to provide more comfort. As Philippa reclines the electric chair to take Kenny's legs off the floor, Shogun comes trotting in from the garden, sees the OH man and barks aggressively, ignoring Philippa's command to be quiet. The OH man backs away.

Kenny joins in with the dog's barking, pleased when Shogun barks back. They have some sort of conversation. Shogun's wagging tail and Kenny's broad grin suggest they've shared a joke.

There is a heavy knock on the door followed by a moment's silence as Shogun goes quiet before barking more aggressively. Kenny asks who it is, and Philippa goes to see. The OH man takes the chair next to Kenny and asks, calmly, how he's feeling and whether he's getting out much. Kenny tells him he goes up the shops or bank nearly every day, when he's not gardening, working on his Triumph or decorating the front room, oh, and on the last Thursday of every month he has to go to the town hall to pay the rates and, in winter, sometimes order coal. And once every three months he has to go into town to pay his union dues. Then he asks the OH man if he's his brother. When the OH man says no, Kenny starts, 'Tinker, tailor, soldier, sailor ...' but gets confused and ends with pointing a finger at the OH man. 'Beggarman?' which he makes a question.

The OH man looks as confused as Kenny.

Shogun has followed Philippa to the front door. He watches as a delivery man drops a week's worth of shopping on the step and appears to listen intently as the man explains about the substitution – a jar of mango chutney instead of bananas. Of course.

The OH man reclines Kenny's chair a little further then goes to help bring through the shopping, ignoring Philippa's protest. Shogun is ok with the OH man now. As they go into the kitchen the washing machine beeps loudly, signalling the end of one of that day's washes. The sound is intrusive enough that Philippa feels obliged to stop unpacking the food delivery to turn off the machine and open its door.

It's a beautiful early summer day and the large kitchen window is south-facing. The kitchen is clearly lit by sunshine. Dirty breakfast detritus is piled by the sink, crumbs from the toaster sprinkle the worktop, and a round stain from the bottom of a cup of coffee is next to the open coffee jar, the lid discarded to one side.

Kenny calls something from the lounge and Philippa shouts back, 'Tea's coming, Dad,' as she puts on the kettle.

'Busy morning,' says the OH man.

'Just the usual,' says Philippa, 'oh, except Shogun. We're dog-sitting for a few hours. We might take him out later.'

'Does Kenny get out?'

'Not much. Depends on the weather and if he's up for

the palaver.'

'Coping?'

'Who? Dad?' Philippa asks, but even I know that the OH man doesn't mean Kenny.

OH man sips his tea and indicates to a picture of a sunset over an ornate, domed building. 'That's nice.' The picture hangs above the hatch between kitchen and lounge.

Philippa nods agreement, 'It's meant to be Brighton Pavilion,' but doesn't admit that she painted it. She gave it to us as an anniversary present, maybe twenty years ago. We'd spent our honeymoon, 1955, in Brighton. It's a lovely painting and it's such a shame she doesn't take credit.

Shogun trots down the hall then back to the kitchen, stops by the open back door and throws up. It's a watery mixture, bright red in colour, much like raspberry jam. Before Philippa can move to throw Shogun out there is another call from the lounge,

'Beverley! You there? I need the toilet.'

'Who's Beverley?' asks the OH man.

'My mother. Dead, I'm afraid.'

'Beverley!' Kenny shouts louder as Shogun vomits again.

'So, how about some respite?' says the OH man.

It's gone two by the time the house is tidy – albeit just a temporary state. The OH man hadn't stayed long. Kenny sleeps in the recliner. Philippa's in the armchair across the room, sipping tea, nibbling a couple of cream crackers, half watching the afternoon film, paying more attention to the painting of Brighton Pavilion she has taken down from above the hatch and propped up on the mantelpiece. Shogun sits on the sofa, watching for cracker crumbs. I regret not getting Kenny another dog after Blofeld died – or after I died, haha.

The landline shrills. Kenny's not disturbed but Shogun barks as Philippa answers. It's Lewis from next door, Joyce's son. He's at the front door and has been knocking for a minute or two. Perhaps we should have kept the doorbell. Philippa's quick to the door but slow to open it, though her smile is genuine as she invites Lewis in. She calls for Shogun who yaps with joy, wakes Kenny, and sprints to the hall. It must be ten years since I've seen Lewis – though I accept I've been dead for eight of those. He married a Personal Financial Investment Consultant – or, as Kenny called it, an insurance sales lady – who lived down on the coast, so Joyce said. Lewis is in decent shape. His eyes are a lighter shade of blue but still kind, and he has a neatly trimmed beard. He's a little shorter than I remember – shorter than Philippa actually – with the beginnings of a paunch. I like his hair. I'm pretty sure it's all his own, as are his teeth. I had dentures by that age, but they were good ones, not NHS – Kenny insisted I keep my 'sweet smile', and didn't mind paying out though we had to sell his old motorbike. I'd resisted for a long time – he loved that bike – before he eventually sold it without me knowing. I never wanted him to. Lewis looks at Philippa while talking and she matches his gaze; why shouldn't she? Her greying hair is thick and wavy and longer than many her age wear it – did I mention she's fifty-eight and a little heavier than a few years ago? But then aren't we all? Except me, obviously. I believe someone once calculated 'our' weight as 21 grams, but if there's one thing I learnt about science, it's that scientific fact is only true until the next scientific fact comes along to disprove it.

Philippa and Lewis exchange pleasantries while Shogun jumps at him, desperate to be picked up. Lewis wears no jewellery, though I see there is a dent in his left-hand ring finger. Philippa invites him through to say hello to Kenny and gather Shogun's things. I'm not sure that's a good idea. Lewis's mother, Joyce, hasn't seen Kenny in quite a while and I'm not keen on Lewis going back and telling tales. But Kenny's face lights up at another visitor, asking Philippa who he is. Lewis sits on the sofa. He's polite. The conversation's polite. He explains he's moving back in with

Joyce, his mother, for a while, and I fancy I see Philippa's smile broaden just a touch. She has good teeth – apart from the two towards the back she lost last year – and should smile more. She sits upright in her chair. She always had good posture. I notice Lewis glance at her bosom. And why wouldn't he? It's a good bosom. Not too big, and mostly still in the right place, gravitationally speaking. Gravitationally. Is that a word? Philippa would laugh kindly at my use.

When the conversation goes quiet – Philippa isn't a natural at keeping it flowing these days – Lewis asks Kenny how he's doing.

'Holding the rails,' says Kenny.

'Which is a good thing,' Philippa explains.

Lewis laughs and repeats, 'Holding the rails,' to show Kenny he gets it.

'You're my brother,' Kenny says to him. Lewis explains not, before indicating to the picture on the mantelpiece to change subject.

Philippa explains, 'Brighton Pavilion.'

Lewis laughs. 'Thought so. I lived near there, for a short while. Renting a room overlooking the promenade. That's a beautiful sunset. More beautiful than any I actually saw, to be honest.'

'Well, also to be honest,' Philippa lowers her voice, as if sharing a secret, 'the sun doesn't shine from that angle at sunset, no matter the time of year. It's a …' Philippa struggles for the word,

'… interpretation?' finishes Lewis.

'I guess.' Philippa matches his laugh and I realise how much I miss her.

'Which you painted?' Lewis asks.

Of course she did. Of course you did Philippa. Tell him.

'I guess.' Philippa tells him; sort of.

'It's very nice.'

'It's better than nice,' I shout silently as Lewis says

goodbye to Kenny and Philippa sees him out.

Back in the lounge Kenny asks, 'Who was that?'

Philippa explains.

'Did you offer him a cup of tea?'

That's a good question. Philippa, why not?

'No, but he liked the Brighton Pavilion painting.' Philippa takes it from the mantelpiece and lays it in Kenny's lap. 'Remember this place, Dad?'

'Sort of.'

'Remember your honeymoon? Brighton. Nineteen fifty-five?' she asks.

'Sort of.'

He's hedging his bets. I remember. We were married on a Friday in April. It was a hastily arranged wedding. A couple of weeks earlier my mother had caught me and Kenny in her own bed on a Saturday afternoon – she came home early with a headache when she was supposed to be working overtime at the bearing factory. She didn't tell my dad why she was so keen to rush arrangements, but she was terrified I'd fall pregnant before being wed. Or, rather: she was terrified of what the neighbours would say. Though, of course, announcing the wedding at such short notice meant they all suspected I was pregnant anyway.

Our wedding was a joyful day and we spent the first night in a cheap hotel in Victoria before catching the train down to Brighton next morning. We had five days in a guest house on the sea front; a real treat, and the sea view was an extravagant gesture by my uncle who paid for it.

For our forty-fifth wedding anniversary, Philippa gave us this painting of Brighton Pavilion. The picture brings happy memories.

Philippa rests the picture back on the mantelpiece. Hanging on the wall directly above it is another of Philippa's paintings. It's much bigger, and deserving of its place. It's another sunset, over the cathedral in Palma, Mallorca, though we spelled it with a 'J' back in those days. Philippa and Ciaran went there for their honeymoon, in nineteen eighty. It's a beautiful painting, though following Philippa's confession about Brighton Pavilion I'm now wondering if the sunset ever does light the honey-beige stone, bricks and spires of the grand building in that way. I've never seen the cathedral – except for pictures – which is a sudden sadness. I'm not into any 'glory to God' nonsense – my God doesn't need to be worshipped – but it is a glorious cathedral and just taking a minute to study the painting can lift my spirits; I imagine what the real thing might do. And now I'm disappointed that I'll never know.

Philippa and Ciaran spent ten days on Mallorca. They were young, Philippa was barely twenty when they married, but I didn't mind. Ciaran was loud, but not pushy, and funny, but not hurtful. At first I worried they'd end up with a houseful of Catholic kids they couldn't afford, but they'd not had so much as one. Philippa never talked to me about it, nor Kenny. I was sad, for them more than us. As far as I could tell, for many years, they got on well, were never apart. They'd finish each other's sentences and choose each other's food in restaurants. They dressed to match – not in the sense of colours, but in the way they complemented each other's style. She would never wear jeans if he was in smart trousers, and he would never wear chinos or trainers if she was in a smart skirt or what he called a 'proper frock'. And she often wore 'proper frocks'. They were a tall, good-looking couple and I still don't know what went wrong.

The last time I saw Ciaran was at my cremation. He stood next to Philippa, but they didn't talk much. Ciaran wrote Kenny a nice letter soon after they got divorced.

Philippa replaces Palma cathedral with Brighton Pavilion. They are both good paintings. She's a talented painter – I think – but rarely picks up a brush these days. I think there's an unfinished portrait in her room but I don't know who it will be.

'Who was that?' asks Kenny again as Philippa flicks through the TV channels.

'That just left? Lewis. He's moving in next door while

33

looking for his own place.'

'Is he my brother?'

'No, Dad. John and Freddy are your brothers.'

'Where are they?'

'John died in the war, Dad. We haven't heard from Freddy in years.'

'Oh. Where's my Beverley?'

'Not with us, Dad.'

'Oh.'

'Where is she?'

'Gone.'

'Is she coming back?'

'No, Dad.'

I look away, catching a sob. Watching over is hard.

'Oh. Where's your husband?' Kenny asks without looking away from the telly.

'We got divorced. Years ago. It's just me and you, now.'

Kenny looks sad and says, 'Me and you.'

Philippa smiles. 'Yep, me and you. Just …' and breaks into song, 'Me and my shadow …'

'Strolling down the avenue,' sings Kenny,

'Me and my shadow …'

'Not a soul to …' Kenny forgets the words and hums the rest.

Philippa bends over him in the chair and cuddles him as best she can. Kenny hugs back.

Chapter 5
Saturday 15ᵗʰ June
Pussy Cat, Pussy Cat

Yesterday was Philippa's birthday. She told Kenny she was fifty-nine – hard to believe, not that I'm suggesting she was telling porkies. But that makes me – never mind, it's as irrelevant as it's possible to be; I've not aged a day in the last eight years, haha. No card from Ciaran. I suppose it was getting on for eight years ago they divorced, shortly after I died. I check the mantelpiece again. There are few cards. I exaggerate – four cards isn't even *few*. It's a sign both of how *few* relatives we have left and how *few* friends Philippa has kept up with. There was a time she and Ciaran were proper social butterflies, but it's been hard for her to keep it up. How would she have time?

I liked Ciaran – did I say that already? I repeat myself but there's no one to remind me. He was cheerful and bright. The first time she brought him home I saw the spark between them. Actually, not so much a spark, but a sharing: laughter; stories; touches unseen – they thought; easy agreement, even, or especially, when perhaps they didn't. They made an effort. She was not quite out of her teens, he not much more. He was lucky to meet her and knew it. I don't know what went wrong, but it was probably when I was falling progressively more ill. I expect they thought they were doing me a favour with their secrets – which is fair, except it was frustrating at the time to feel something was not right, and even more frustrating now to not be able to ask. The subject occasionally comes up in conversation with Kenny, when he notices the wedding photo still on the sideboard.

'I know him,' Kenny may say, nodding towards the tarnished silver framed photograph on the sideboard. 'He's my brother.'

'No, Dad,' says Philippa.

'Sure?'

Philippa nods.

'Who is he?'

'Ciaran,' says Philippa.

'That's a church.' Kenny studies the photograph. 'Is he your husband?'

'Not anymore.' Philippa is factual.

'Is he dead?'

'No, Dad.'

'What happened?'

'We stopped laughing, Dad,' Philippa says cryptically. She gives nothing away, not even to a man who will forget within the minute; at least, not when that man is her dad.

'Me and Beverely haven't.'

'Haven't what, Dad?'

'Stopped laughing. Where is she?'

My heart breaks. Again.

Philippa hesitates, '... just popped out, Dad. You'll laugh when you're back together.'

Kenny looks confused but says nothing.

Back together? I wonder if that's how it works. Please, God.

It's true, we laughed a great deal. Mostly over very little. Often over a memory that wasn't funny at the time but which one of us would bring out when the moment was right, or when he wanted to steady my nerves, or remind me how much he loved me, or we were telling stories to others which proved our history, our love. One favourite was the night of our eighth date. After a late show down the Odeon – *Doctor In The House*, Dirk Bogarde, of course – he took me home on his Thunderbird, careful in the rain on the greasy roads, it was a powerful bike. He came in for a cuppa, he'd already met my parents, and we sat in the front parlour for a while, cuddling lightly but kissing hard, resisting the urge to get carried away – no pawing, my dad was likely to walk in without knocking. I had one ear cocked to the door which spoiled the moment, and when Mum started making a lot of noise washing up the tea cups, I knew they were going to bed. Kenny said he'd better be leaving. But his bike wouldn't start. It was raining hard and he stood next to my dad at the open front door, discussing what was most likely: water in the electrics or in the fuel. They both knew about that stuff – my dad worked in engineering; he would have been so proud of Philippa becoming a draughtsperson – and I could tell my dad respected Kenny's opinion. And they could have talked all night, but it wouldn't make the bike start. Mum said Kenny had missed the last bus and Kenny said he could walk and Mum said that didn't make sense, he'd have to stop over, and Dad probably caught my eye catching Kenny's, so Dad lightly, but firmly – it was a knack he had – suggested that as we only had two bedrooms Mum and I would have the double-bed, Dad would have my single, and Kenny would be in the same bedroom as him, on a camp bed. And, as Dad suggested – lightly but firmly again – the only reason any of us had to get out of bed was to visit the bathroom, which was in the lean-to extension out back downstairs. The bathroom was always cold despite being new, but far better than the little shed we used to have down the bottom of the garden.

Kenny forever had the joke that the first night we slept under the same roof, he was closer to my dad than me, and, 'Bloody hell, could your dad snore and fart, often at the same time.' And it was always funny. In the morning, I'd gone down to the kitchen before him, to make sure he saw me in my best nightdress. Mum suggested I put on my dressing gown. I said it was in the wash. She said she knew, because she saw me put it there first thing, together with my old nightdress. Dad frowned and left for work. That was something else we laughed about for years after.

I'd thought Philippa and Ciaran had laughed a lot too. Maybe not, at least towards the end; both mine and theirs, I suppose.

Anyway, yesterday was Philippa's birthday. I watch as she wanders from the lounge, Kenny is asleep – to the kitchen, the washing-up is already put away – to the garden, the clothes line has been cleared but it's still too wet after last night's shower to cut the grass – to Kenny's bedroom, the bed linen has been changed – upstairs to her own bedroom, I catch a glimpse of that half-started, not half-finished, painting on an easel. I don't go in; it's one of my rules. I hear Philippa plump a pillow and spray some air freshener, then back to the kitchen, too early to start preparations for that night's ready-meal – she goes into the lounge, Kenny still sleeps, and with no Sky TV Philippa can't watch *The Sopranos* again. Carmela was our favourite character. Philippa takes the latest bank statement from a pile of opened post. She looks at it, goes to her purse, takes out some receipts and ticks them off on the statement. She accounts for every penny. Money is tight. She glances at the phone, as if considering who to ring, then looks away. She could make a start on the ironing but that is beyond boring – to the downstairs bathroom, it's been cleaned since that morning's 'toileting' disaster; a 'code brown' calling for mop and bucket. Thank goodness there is lino rather than carpet in there. Philippa makes a note on the pad on the kitchen top: Amazon, new mop head, disposable gloves, bleach. She wanders up the hall to look in the mirror. Her hair needs a trim. She wonders aloud if Joyce, or maybe Lewis, would babysit – no, not babysit, sit with – Kenny while she pops to the hairdressers. Perhaps a trim would make her look a bit younger? Or perhaps growing it longer would? Apart from her dad, there's no one's opinion to be asked. She could ask Lewis? I think it needs a trim, but then a mother almost always does. To the front room, rarely used – does it really need a vacuum? Philippa goes back to the broom cupboard in the kitchen for the Hoover. She's looking so hard for something to do. When you're busy all day, it's hard not to be. She vacuums the front room, checks the car insurance renewal date, orders a birthday card for Cousin

Martin from the internet – even though he didn't send one to her – cooks up a batch of Bolognese for a couple of meals, and examines the disconnected wiring where the old doorbell used to be. Part of me hopes she's going to put it back up.

I suppose all those tasks are a form of companion. I tell her to sit down, watch some tennis – Wimbledon is on, ladies final today, I think – read a book, continue that painting – I want to know whose portrait it will be, it might turn out to be David Essex, she was besotted as a teenager – watch an old episode of *Dad's Army*, bound to be on one of the Freeview channels. Kenny and I used to love that:

'Don't tell him your name, Pike!'

We'd laughed so hard. Philippa had been perhaps thirteen at the time, sitting with us in the lounge, not getting it. That made us laugh even harder. I laughed easily and often. So did Kenny. Did I say that earlier? I miss laughing with him.

Philippa looks at my photo next to the toaster and smiles. Or do I imagine that?

I am pregnant in the photo, but not showing. I think it was the day after we told my mum and dad, barely three months after we married.

'Well that was close then,' Mum had said, not smiling. Dad frowned, perhaps guessing what she meant. I went with Kenny to the bar to buy Mum a vodka and orange and Dad a pint of Mackeson to celebrate. Mum downed her drink in one, said she wasn't ready to be a nan yet, and went back up to the bar to order another round and, '… get some bleedin' pork scratchings.' She'd never sworn or eaten pork scratchings before. Even Dad laughed.

I lost that baby a week or two after the photo. 'Lost'. What a stupid word for it. I have always believed it would have been a boy, so we chose the name Sasha. I don't know why, but it seemed to fit. I wanted something different, special, neither fashionable nor old; something that we would never confuse with someone else. He would be the only Sasha that Kenny and I could ever think about on hearing the name.

It took a long time, but eventually, and for years afterwards, whenever we remembered Mum's reaction in the bar we laughed. It was better than crying about the loss; except of course we were.

In the 70s there was a famous French singer with that name, and for a while the radios were full of 'Raindrops Keep Fallin' On My Head' in a romantic French accent. I cried every time it played. I never told Philippa why.

Philippa and Ciaran never had children, never talked about it. How is it I never asked? How was I unable to? A mother should talk to her daughter about everything. I wanted to. I think she wanted to. I think we were both scared of upsetting each other – which I guess is a way of showing love, isn't it?

I remember once, when Ciaran came round for tea, the two of them were quiet; didn't finish each other's sentences, or brush against each other as much as usual. After tea, I washed and Philippa dried. I asked, tentatively, if anything was wrong but she insisted nothing. When they were leaving I noticed he rested a hand on her tummy and she frowned. To this day, I wonder.

Philippa would have been a good mum. And a child would have been the best of company for her – I know – and a child, an adult by now, could have been here today, watching Wimbledon with her. Who knows? That child might have been a tennis player or a scientist or an actress or Prime Minister or a famous singer or, best of all, simply a friend.

Philippa replaces the Hoover in the cupboard – it's actually a Vax but I can't get out of the habit – and goes back to the lounge, making sufficient noise to disturb Kenny, whose half-open eyes peer over the top of his spectacles. Kenny smiles, 'I know you. You're my Philippa.'

'Of course.'

'Good. Is that cat back?' Kenny indicates to the garden.

'Can't see it, Dad.' Philippa stands at the patio doors.

'What's that black thing? Down the bottom.'

'Not a cat, Dad. Is it a shadow under a bush? I've seen a white cat now and again, but not black.'

'Bloody cats. Messing on the grass.'

'I don't think they do, Dad. You used to shoot a water pistol at them, remember?'

'Did I?' Kenny laughs. I don't. I didn't know he shot a water pistol at the cats that occasionally wandered into the garden. I quite liked them. They filled a gap when Blofeld died. I even used to put cat food down for them, but never told Kenny.

'You're a naughty man,' Philippa tells him and laughs, wiping dribble from his chin.

Kenny looks pleased with himself and recites, 'Pussy cat, pussy cat, where have you been? I've been to London to visit the queen.'

Philippa adds, 'Pussy cat, pussy cat, what did you there?' and prompts Kenny to finish.

'I frightened a little mouse under a chair.'

Philippa takes a pad of paper and a pencil from my old sewing chest and sketches a cartoon of a frightened mouse and scary cat, eyes narrowed to slits, fangs showing. There are only a few lines on the paper but the image is instantly recognisable. She has a talent. They both laugh harder. I do too, now. How could I not?

Kenny stops laughing suddenly. 'Where's Beverley?'

'Gone, Dad.'

'Where?'

Philippa hesitates before telling him. 'She's dead, Dad. Eight years ago.'

'Oh. We said we'd not leave each other behind,' Kenny says, frowning.

That was true, we did say that. Philippa nods, as if she understands, encouraging Kenny to speak.

'I was meant to keep her safe. I didn't. I said I'd go with her.' Kenny's watery eyes are more watery still.

'You did all you could, Dad.'

'I didn't keep my promise.'

That was also true. He didn't, couldn't, fulfil the promise we'd made to each other. For a while I resented that. But I'm over it now and hope he doesn't explain to Philippa what the promise would have meant. I dread to think what it might have done to Philippa if she was the one that found us. And it won't help her now to know our plans. Kenny wipes a tear from his cheek, 'I miss her.'

'Me too.' Philippa rubs Kenny's arm. 'I miss my mum. I miss her smile. It made so much right.'

I miss me too, but no one can rub my arm. I miss Kenny, though he's right there. What do I miss most? Laughing, cuddling, making love, having sex – not at all the same thing – sitting quietly, watching a film, walking Blofeld, arguing about what film to watch; our joint, mutual, exhausting worrying about Philippa – always that worry; still, for me; not so much for Kenny now.

'Where's the dog?' Kenny asks.

'Blofeld?' Philippa hesitates again. 'He's about somewhere.'

Kenny falls asleep. I see Philippa going through her mental to-do list again. Her eyes settle on the pile of ironing in the corner. She's irritated by the interruption of the telephone. It's the OH man, calling on a Saturday? It's the third time he's called in the last couple of weeks.

'Respite? How much will it cost?' Philippa asks. I can't hear the answer but Philippa looks thoughtful before saying, slowly and with a hint of disbelief, 'And Social Services pay towards it?' The OH man says something and Philippa says, with little conviction, 'I'll give it some thought.'

Philippa finishes the ironing, hunts the kitchen drawers for a battery for the hall clock which stopped yesterday, and lays the table for the evening meal. They will eat early. Kenny hasn't eaten since his late breakfast. She wakes him gently.

'Toilet, Dad?' Philippa asks, but it's just for information. The smell tells Philippa that it's too late. She won't let Kenny eat in soiled pants.

Philippa brings in the wheeled commode and goes back out to bring in the hoist, then goes back out again to get the disposable gloves and bin-bag she forgot first time. The sling is slipped around Kenny's chest and under his arm. There is a sharp intake of breath – of course – as the hoist lifts him. While Kenny's in the air his trousers are removed; he's embarrassed. Sometimes he isn't, sometimes he is. I wish he never was. It serves no purpose and he deserves better. Philippa carefully checks the contents of the incontinence pants though the smell is all we need to know. Philippa tears the pants at their perforated side seams so she doesn't have to pull them down and over Kenny's feet – that would be tricky to do considering the contents. She folds the pants in on themselves, deftly capturing the contents, thank goodness it wasn't a loose movement, and puts them in the disposable bag, tying it tightly shut. Not once does she pull a face at the smell. She works quickly – Kenny is still suspended – and lowers him to the commode.

'Oooh, that's cold,' says Kenny.

'We need to invent a heated toilet seat, Dad,' says Philippa.

Kenny laughs as if for the first time and says, 'I should coco.'

Philippa takes him out of the lounge, through the kitchen and into the downstairs bathroom. Fifteen minutes later she has wiped, cleaned, dressed and taken Kenny into the kitchen.

I had to wipe and clean Kenny once. Once was enough. Not because I minded – he was much younger then and I was, still am, his wife – but he hated the indignity. It was a long time ago. His appendix burst and it hurt, a great deal. I know that, 'cos he was moaning with pain and in those days he was indestructible. But after the op, when he was bedridden and desperate for a number two, and all the nurses were busy, I helped him with the bedpan. I know he was desperate 'cos no way else would he have asked me. We never talked about it again. It was never a story to laugh about. Dignity might have a price, but its loss costs far more.

Philippa holds his dignity dear, I'm sure, and he seems to understand.

While she sanitises her hands, flinching as the gel finds a small cut in a finger, I think she's considering whether to leave Kenny in the commode while they eat dinner, albeit properly covered. She decides not to – I knew she wouldn't – and takes him in the commode back to the lounge to use the hoist, redress him and transfer him back to the wheelchair and then back to the kitchen.

There are no quick tasks anymore. Everything is a two-person job really. Nothing is easy.

I'd say I'm physically exhausted just watching, but that's just meaningless, patronising and not even true. I am never tired, and yet do not have the energy to do anything, haha.

Except weep for them.

When Kenny's sitting at the table she returns the commode, and then the hoist, back to the bedroom. Kenny has fallen asleep.

Philippa chooses ready meals – cottage pie for Kenny, fish and chips for herself – and prepares a pot of tea while the microwave is spinning. She wakes Kenny to eat, singing, 'Pussy cat, pussy cat …'

'… where have you been?' finishes Kenny who has to be reminded, several times, how to hold the cutlery and to eat before it goes cold.

There is a game show on the TV but neither pays attention even though I am shouting out answers. Philippa is flicking through a hairstyle magazine. She has been flicking through this same magazine for at least three months. Magazines are ridiculously expensive these days. So are haircuts. I wonder if that's partly why it's been so long since Philippa had a cut, let alone some colour put in to hide the grey wisps.

Kenny stops eating to pick at some food he has dropped in his lap. Philippa curses under her breath – she forgot the bib, which she now puts around Kenny. He doesn't want it. I don't blame him. He's not a child. Philippa ignores him. I don't blame her either. He's really just a child. It's another half-hour before Kenny has finished eating, fed in part by Philippa. It's another five minutes to wheel him back to the lounge, bring the hoist from the bedroom – why did she take it back there? I think I know why. She's desperate not to turn the lounge into an extension of the 'ward' – and transfer Kenny to the riser/recliner. Kenny looks at the TV but doesn't watch. Philippa hands him his Tommee Tippee cup and a chocolate biscuit before returning the hoist to the bedroom. She goes back to the kitchen to clear up the mess, do the washing-up, clean the floor, and make another pot of tea.

'Beverley!'

Philippa doesn't hear the first call over the boiling kettle.

'Beverley!' Kenny tries again.

'In a minute, Dad,' she calls back as the kettle subsides.

'Beverley!' Louder and a touch desperate.

'In a minute!'

'Beverley, Beverley!'

'What!' Philippa screams as she returns to the lounge.

'Beverley?' Kenny questions.

'No, Dad,' Philippa snaps, 'I'm … what have you done?' She spits the question, accusing.

Kenny has somehow managed to pry the top from the Tommee Tippee cup. Orange squash soaks into his jumper and trousers and seeps into the chair's fabric. Kenny holds up his hands, they are covered in melted chocolate, the remnants of the biscuit are on the floor.

'Jesus, Dad, what the …'

Philippa takes a breath and spins away, her face

reddening, and slaps a hand down hard on my sewing cabinet.

'I need the toilet,' pleads Kenny.

'For God's sake, Dad! Why …'

Philippa takes another breath and holds it this time. So do I – or at least I would if I could.

Kenny looks at her, puppy-like, pitiful. I look at her, shocked then distraught. She's crying silently as she leaves the room, 'Give me a minute, Dad … a minute.'

I don't know what to do, so I stay with Kenny.

Later, after Kenny is sorted, Philippa sits in the armchair next to him. As the early evening news starts she asks quietly, 'Shall I ring the OH man on Monday, Dad?'

Kenny snores.

Chapter 6
Monday 24th June
Rebecca

'Knees up Mother Brown, knees up Mother Brown …' sings Kenny as Philippa wheels him into the lounge. Philippa joins in for the rest of the song which has to be finished – Kenny will not accept the song being incomplete – and waits for Philippa to laugh at the end before he, too, laughs. It's coming up to one. Kenny is toileted, washed and dressed. The bathroom is spotless and everything in its place. Breakfast is finished. The washing-up is done and draining. Kenny's bed linen has been changed. Philippa has vacuumed downstairs – she was up at six thirty this morning – and Kenny's ready to be settled in the lounge. With luck there will be some birds at the feeder.

Philippa transfers Kenny to the riser/recliner using the hoist, settles him comfortably – as far as she can tell; the cushion squeezed and bunched at his back for extra support never looks comfy – returns the hoist to the bedroom, checks her watch, pops out to the garden to untangle a sheet drying on the clothesline, and sprays a day's worth of chemical air freshener around all rooms.

How is 'blue sunshine satin' a smell?

It's a big day and she does not want – won't have – their visitor thinking them slovenly. With Kenny and the house 'ready', Philippa changes from jeans into a floral summer dress I haven't seen since last year. I can't remember the last time Philippa treated herself to something new to wear. Good clothes are so expensive and she always said, 'Buy cheap, buy twice.' Fortunately, the dress fits even better this summer. Looking after Kenny is a daily workout and ready meals are not so appetising. The dress stops just below her knees. She puts on mascara and lipstick and pinches her cheeks, then musses her hair until it's fashionably untidy. It's good to see her making the effort, even if it is only for a trip to the shops.

With the patio doors open, Kenny has a good view out to the garden. I can hear children from the school over the back. It must be lunchbreak and the laughing, squealing and shouting carries to the lounge. Kenny smiles; I hope because he hears the happy kids. It's a bright day with a few scattered, wispy clouds lying like creases on a cloth – the blue sky can almost be described as satin-like, haha.

Kenny's attention is caught by a dog barking. I think it's Shogun. We hear Lewis calling for him to stop. It sounds like Lewis is chasing the dog up the passage between our two houses and out to the front. Philippa, being nosey – and why not? – goes to Kenny's bedroom at the front so she can look out. Lewis is standing on Joyce's drive next door, screaming for Shogun to come back, but the dog's twenty yards down the road, having chased a cat onto a car roof. It's a black cat. Perhaps Kenny did see one in the garden the other day. The cat hisses at the stupid dog while it frantically circles and jumps uselessly at the car. Philippa watches Lewis. He's wearing a smart business suit and carrying a briefcase, not much good for chasing dogs. There's something different about his hair and the beard has gone. Philippa shouts to Kenny that she'll only be a moment and joins Lewis out front, making sure to leave the door on the latch. I follow Philippa out but stay on the porch.

'Bloody dog,' says Lewis, taking another, ever so slightly longer, look at Philippa. 'Mum's gone out and I'm gonna be late for an interview. First one since I came back.' It's a sunny day and there's a sheen of sweat on his forehead. It's lovely and warm out here, if only I could feel it. I never feel warm these days. I miss it. I could leave the porch's shade, slip into the sun, a little further from the house, that might help, but it's been such a long time and, well, it's been a long time, hasn't it? Besides, I can see and hear fine from here.

'Don't worry, you go, I'll get Shogun,' says Philippa, 'and good luck with the interview. You …' she hesitates and

I hope she may be going to tell him how nice he looks and that the job's as good as his, '… will do fine, I'm sure.'

Philippa, Philippa, Philippa. Is that all you have? Lewis thanks her. As she starts towards Shogun, an orange Mini – old school, very small, very orange, proper Mini – pulls up outside our house, its tinny radio plays 'Dancing Queen'. I know they're a bit after my time, but I do like some Abba, though they're no Andrews Sisters, never mind Cliff and The Shadows. A petite, but not skinny, pale woman athletically eases her way from behind the tight driver's seat, takes in the scene of a West Highland Terrier barking furiously up at a defiant cat, and joins Lewis and Philippa.

'Have you tried a biscuit?' asks the woman, smiling. I can't place her accent. It has more than a touch of eastern Europe, though my experience of such accents is limited, to say the least. It could be Romanian or Hungarian or Polish, for all I know. Or even from Montenegro. I only learnt of Montenegro the other day. Kenny and Philippa were watching a James Bond film I hadn't seen before: *Casino Royale*.

'A biscuit? To distract the dog or coax the cat?' Philippa asks the woman, returning the smile.

The woman laughs easily and loudly. Now that she's standing next to Philippa she seems even shorter, but carries herself as tall as she can. She wears dark blue, calf-length slacks and a blouse of bright blue with amber sleeves, cuffs turned up just a couple of times. Her hair is short and blonde, very blonde, and I suspect dyed though I can't see the roots from here. Nor can I see her face well, so I notice instead she wears canvas sandals that have two-inch block heels. The blue polish on her toenails nearly matches the blouse and her fingernails are bright yellow. She loops the strap of a satchel over her shoulder to hang across her chest, looks behind Philippa to the house and asks, 'Number twelve?' pointing to our front door, on which is clearly visible the number.

Philippa nods to the woman then suggests again to

Lewis that he can go, she'll sort out Shogun and the cat. Lewis is thankful. Philippa and the stranger watch him leave, then the stranger says, 'I'm Kaska. I'm here for Mr. Cooper.'

'Hi. We're ready for you,' says Philippa. An odd way to describe it.

'Nice to meet you,' says Kaska.

'Mr. Cooper … Kenny … is indoors.'

'Shall we sort out the dog first? Or the cat?' Kaska laughs.

It's fortunate we live in a quiet road. Philippa walks towards Shogun, calling his name. Kaska is just behind her. But Shogun will not be distracted from the excitement at having trapped a cat, and I doubt he hears his name being called over his own barking. He stands with his front paws on the car's bumper, desperate to get closer to the black cat which has stopped hissing and now sneers down at the stupid dog with disdain. Can a cat sneer? I don't know, but frankly, it's just as the dog deserves. One of the neighbours across the street has come out to see what's happening. Philippa waves at her, as if this is completely normal. I notice that Kaska, smiling broadly, also waves to the neighbour. Philippa creeps up behind Shogun – not difficult because he's so focused – and makes a grab for him, but isn't close enough for a proper hold, and the surprisingly strong and determined little dog wriggles free. He bolts for the back of the car. Philippa curses but, conscious of her audience – the neighbour's husband has joined her at the door – pretends it's normal to be kneeling in the road, nearly headbutting an old Ford Fiesta's bonnet. Kaska walks cautiously round to the back of the car, calling, 'Choking, Choking,' which is close to his name, and makes Philippa smile as she pushes herself to standing and goes round the car the other way – a pincer movement. Shogun doesn't care. The cat has turned to look down at Shogun, teasing the dog into a frenzy. Philippa and Kaska reach the end of the car at the same time. Kaska puts her finger to her mouth, urging quiet, but looks close to bursting into yet more laughter. Shogun sees them, but the cat is the prize. Philippa and Kaska gradually close in on the dog from both sides. When barely a foot away, they both lunge, but Shogun is too quick again. He's under the car and back up to the front before Kaska and Philippa can steady their balance. The neighbours laugh. So do I.

Kaska frowns, hunts through her satchel and pulls out a Milky Way – a small one, the sort we get in the Christmas tin of Celebrations. Kenny's favourite is Galaxy Caramel, even though the goo gets stuck under his denture. Kaska shows the chocolate to Philippa. 'Biscuit, no. But chocolate? Oh yes.' Kaska laughs and throws it to Philippa. Philippa waits until she's close to Shogun, back at the car's front bumper, and makes as much noise as she can unwrapping the bite-size bar. Even Shogun is distracted by that sound. Philippa unwraps it slowly, theatrically. Shogun wants this, but he also wants the cat. He looks from chocolate to cat and back and decides the cat is going nowhere. Philippa pretends to eat the sweet and makes a sucking sound. Shogun takes a step towards her. She shows him the chocolate. This is too much. He lunges at her fingers, she drops it with a shriek, and Kaska, who has crept up from the other side, grabs Shogun's collar. Job done. Shogun gulps the chocolate in one go and wriggles furiously in Kaska's tight arms but cannot escape. He barks angrily over her shoulder as he's carried away, Kaska trying to stroke him to calmness. The cat looks over its own shoulder, almost shrugs – can a cat shrug? – and starts to wash itself.

Philippa leads the way into the house, taking Shogun from Kaska, and calling to Kenny, 'I'm back, Dad. We have visitors.'

The hall falls into shadow as Philippa closes the front door. She lowers Shogun to the floor. He scrabbles to get away from her and rushes through to see Kenny. Philippa carefully brushes something from her knee and winces – I see a small mark from when she knelt heavily on the road. Standing to full height, she turns to Kaska and offers a hand,

'Hi, I'm Philippa, Mr. Cooper ... Kenny's, daughter.' Now that they are no longer trying to catch Shogun, Philippa is formal and a touch nervous.

'Nice to meet you, I'm Kaska.'

'Kaska,' Philippa repeats. Kaska nods.

Shogun is barking loudly and Kenny is shouting something unintelligible but not unfriendly. Philippa shows Kaska through to the back lounge.

Shogun and Kenny are playing tug of war with a handkerchief. The little dog is almost pulling Kenny out of the chair, but he's not worried and laughs heartily. He holds the handkerchief tightly in one hand while the other tries to keep in his top denture plate, which is close to falling out.

Philippa calls to Kenny but he's too busy playing with Shogun. Philippa calls again, twice, with no response, so she goes to the open patio doors, shouts, 'Shogun! Cat! Cat! Go boy! Go!' and takes half a step onto the patio. Shogun knows where his duty lies and lets go of the handkerchief to burst outside, barking excitedly, and desperate to find the imaginary intruder – I expect he believes it will be the same black cat, and the recent humiliation at the car must be repaid, violently. Philippa returns to Kenny. He's fumbled his denture back into place. Philippa takes a tissue from the box permanently on the small coffee table next to the riser/recliner and dabs his chin. Philippa shaved him this morning but I notice a small patch of stubble was missed.

'Dad, this is Kaska.'

Kenny looks to Kaska, standing to the side of the chair. She drops gracefully to her haunches to be head height and offers her hand, 'Mr Cooper, nice to meet you.' Her accent is thick and musical.

There is doubt in Kenny's eyes but he wants Kaska to like him, so he matches her smile. I hope his denture will stay in place. They shake hands but he looks to Philippa, who nods reassuringly.

'Kaska's going to keep you company while I pop up the shops. I won't be long.'

'How are you?' Kaska asks him.

Kenny looks confused but still smiles and answers, 'Holding the rails.'

Philippa passes the Tommee Tippee cup, encouraging him to drink while, '... I show Kaska around.'

Philippa shows her the bathroom, where the incontinence pants, disposable gloves and other toileting paraphernalia are stored, then the kitchen with kettle, tea, coffee, sugar, fridge, biscuits – Kenny's afternoon treat is due in less than an hour – then to the bedroom to show the hoist and commode, though Philippa's not expecting her to use them even though Kaska assures Philippa she has been trained on that model, then back to the lounge for the riser/recliner control, TV remote control and a run through of Kenny's favourite programmes and a mention that he's not due any tablets until tea-time. Philippa leaves little to chance. Kaska smiles and nods patiently, occasionally asking a question, though I suspect more for Philippa's benefit than hers. Kenny watches and asks Kaska, 'Who are you?'

'Kaska. I will be with you for a short time.' She offers her hand to shake again. Kenny accepts but asks Philippa,

'Do I know her?'

'You might do, Dad.'

Which seems a bit of a cop out answer to me. Kaska is booked in for two respite sessions – today and Wednesday – to see if it works out. Social Services will pay half the cost, leaving Kenny and Philippa to find the rest, so they need to be sure it's worth it. Kaska excuses herself to use the bathroom and, as she leaves the lounge, Kenny says to Philippa, 'She talks funny.'

Kaska will have heard and Philippa blushes. 'You can't say that, Dad,' and looks to the door where Kaska has stopped. She's still smiling but neither I nor Philippa know her well enough to tell if she's offended.

'Why not?' asks Kenny. He can't see that Kaska is still there.

'Because,' says Philippa, leaving Kenny and going to

Kaska to apologise. Kaska raises a hand to indicate it's not a problem and says, 'But aren't you meant to be going out for an hour? It's why I'm here. And Choking is back to help.' She motions to the patio door. Shogun strolls in, happy at having accomplished something.

Philippa hesitates. 'It's ... I've never ... left Dad before.'

This isn't exactly true. When she first moved in to look after Kenny, and he was able to get about with a frame and didn't need incontinence wear, she would leave Kenny to go shopping or to teach at the art class. I think she means it's the first time she's left Kenny with someone else.

'You're not leaving him. You are coming back, right?' Kaska jokes. 'Really, don't worry.'

Philippa doesn't know Kaska, and I wish I could tell her it will be all right, I'll be here. Though, tell the truth, I'm a little worried too. I don't know Kaska either, and she does, to use Kenny's phrase, 'talk funny'. I hope he won't be rude, and I realise that worries me more than leaving him with a complete stranger. I stare into Kaska's face – of course she doesn't know – and it's the sort of thing I used to be embarrassed to do, but eight years on I find it's one of the few advantages of being dead, along with never catching a nasty cold, stubbing a toe on the bed frame, plucking my eyebrows or checking for unusual lumps, bumps and new moles. Kaska has a small face with pale, clear skin stretched tightly over high, sharp cheekbones. There is a scar over her right eye, maybe quarter of an inch. Her smile is broad – perhaps wider than suits her face – with white, nearly straight teeth; nearly as straight as my dentures. She has light frown and laugh lines and a little pinching around her mouth – I wonder if she smokes, and I wonder if she's older than I first thought. No matter, she's very attractive. But what makes her 'watchable' are her eyes. They are green and alive. I stare at them, at her, until she blinks.

'Really, you can go,' continues Kaska, 'it will be all right. I believe Choking will be more trouble. I have only one Milky Way left.' She laughs and goes back to Kenny. 'Mr Cooper, can I call you Kenny?'

Kenny looks to Philippa who nods, as does Kenny.

Yet another person calling him Kenny? I'm not sure I'm happy about that.

'See,' says Kaska to Philippa. 'All good. The shops will be closed by the time you get there. Is your knee all right? Will you need a plaster from the pharmacy?'

The mark on Philippa's knee is more than a bruise, Kaska has noticed what I did not – there is a small graze.

Hesitantly, Philippa gathers her bag from the kitchen and is almost at the front door when she returns to the lounge. Kaska is helping Kenny with his Tommee Tippee cup.

'I forgot. Just in case,' says Philippa, passing to Kaska a slip of paper with her mobile number.

'Of course, just in case,' agrees Kaska.

Philippa is back after forty minutes. She calls out a loud, 'Hello!' as she lets herself in and hears singing from the lounge:

'… knees up, knees up, don't get the breeze up,
knees up Mother Brown.
Oh my what a rotten song,
What a rotten song …'

Kenny leads the singing, Kaska joins in with the bits she remembers; she learnt this song only minutes ago.

Philippa adds her voice as she goes to the lounge and the song concludes with Kenny's customary, 'Oi!' He laughs, proud of himself, as Kaska and Philippa clap.

'Hello, Dad. You've taught Kaska a new song.' Philippa sounds and looks relieved.

'You're my daughter.' He smiles at her, then to Kaska, 'This is my daughter.'

'Of course,' says Kaska.

'Who are you?' Dad asks her.

Kaska doesn't miss a beat. 'I am your friend, Kaska, of course.' She smiles broadly.

'Kaska. Of course.' Repeats Kenny. Then it strikes him as funny. 'Kaska course, Kaska course, courseKaska, KaskcourseKaska.' He laughs. So do we all. He starts wagging his finger around the three of us, chanting, 'Tinker, tailor, soldier, sailor, rich man, poor man, beggarman, thief,' ending at Kaska.

'And which are you? That's another song for you to teach me next time.' Kaska laughs.

Shogun comes in from the garden to see what's going on and, no doubt, in hope that Philippa has brought a treat – he might be stupid, but he's no fool.

'How was it?' Philippa asks Kaska.

I could tell her. I was watching over Kenny. I was here. I could tell her it went well. Kenny was a little confused but Kaska was kind and gentle and chatty; good at asking questions Kenny could follow. He didn't always understand her accent – quite thick at times – but when he put on his 'pretend I get it' smile, Kaska was quick to see his bluff. That's when she started speaking slowly. And she made sure to keep him sipping from his Tommee Tippee cup. She didn't mind – too much – when Shogun started humping her leg and, as far as I could tell, wasn't casing the joint for things to steal. Of course I never thought she would, but you hear the stories. There's a ten-pound note lying on the dresser and it's my job to watch over them. I could tell Philippa all this. I wish I could. I wish with all my heart I could.

I wouldn't tell Philippa that Kenny didn't seem to miss her until Kaska found the old photo album in the book shelf and started looking through some photographs with him – that's when he also missed me.

'That's my Beverley,' he said, pointing me out in our wedding picture. 'That's my Beverley,' he said pointing to me being carried by him out of the sea – Littlehampton, I think. He carried me so easily. He was so strong. I was so light. Even lighter now, haha. 'That's my Beverley,' he said, pointing to the tired face trying to smile for the camera with a tiny Philippa resting on her shoulder. She barely fed or slept for the first fortnight. It was exhausting, for us both. But more than the exhaustion was the worry. What was I doing wrong? Was something wrong with Philippa? I'd already failed with Sasha. Was something wrong with me? It was a worry even worse than when Kenny was rushed in for that emergency appendix removal and I was scared, so scared, he would die on the operating table. But being scared for Philippa was worse, is worse. Being worried for her started that second day and never stopped. No wonder I'm emotionally cream-crackered.

'It went well,' says Kaska, placing a hand gently on Philippa's forearm. 'He's a gentleman. And Choking was a good boy.' She shows Philippa the empty wrapper of a small Milky Way.

Philippa laughs, 'Well, thank you so much,' unpacking her overlarge handbag. Out comes a couple of doughnuts in a paper bag, a tube of Germolene and a battered old paperback, *The Thorn Birds*, that I'm guessing came from the charity shop – she'd be better to find an old copy of *The Carpet Baggers*; proper racy story, and quickly passed round the girls at the cigarette packing factory back in the day. She's not been much of a reader lately, but smells faintly of coffee, so I guess, I hope, she spent some of her break away from Kenny in a café, reading and relaxing, people watching perhaps.

'One thing,' says Kaska, 'I noticed Kenny sometimes has difficulty swallowing, when he was drinking.'

Interesting that Kaska should say that. I'd thought that also.

Philippa sounds a little defensive, 'Really?'

'Not every time. But when sipping for the first time the cup is presented.'

Despite Kaska's accent she's clear in her description – formal even. Seeing something in Philippa's face she adds, 'I thought I'd mention it.'

'Yes, of course,' says Philippa. 'I'll look out for that.'

'Beverley!' Kenny calls over his shoulder to them. 'That you?'

'No, Dad. It's me.' Philippa and Kaska go to him.

'That's my daughter,' Kenny says to Kaska and then asks Philippa, 'Who's that?'

'This is Kaska,' says Philippa.

'She talks funny, doesn't she?'

Philippa looks apologetically at Kaska who shrugs to show she's not offended. That is kind of her and I wonder at what point offence would be, should be, taken? And what happens when that point is reached?

'Don't be … silly, Dad,' says Philippa. 'How about a doughnut? Kaska needs to go and I need to change your pants.'

'It's ok, I toileted Kenny just before you came back. It was not double-soiled,' says Kaska, again using that more formal voice, reminding us that Kenny is, firstly, a patient to be cared for.

'Oh, thank you,' offers Philippa, 'but you needn't. I mean, what with having to faff about with the hoist and everything.'

'Faff?' asks Kaska. 'What is faff?'

But before Philippa can reply, Kenny has started singing 'Knees Up Mother Brown' and we must all join in and sing it to the very end, even though Kaska doesn't know the song. Shogun barks to join in the fun, with one eye on the bag of doughnuts on the table.

'I have to go now, Kenny. See you soon?' says Kaska, making it a question, holding out a hand for Kenny to shake, but trying to catch Philippa's eye as she adds, 'Wednesday, I believe is booked.'

'Of course,' says Philippa, showing Kaska to the front door and saying goodbye with, 'Have a good day.'

I add, 'Get what you can from it. It won't come round again.'

Kaska shakes her hand and gives Shogun, standing obediently by Philippa – he knows where his best chance of a doughnut lays – a scratch behind the ear.

Philippa and Shogun watch Kaska walk to her car then go back to join Kenny.

'She was nice, wasn't she, Dad?' says Philippa as she puts the Tommee Tippee cup to Kenny's lips.

'Who was?' he asks, then sips from the mouthpiece but chokes on the orange squash. Philippa grabs a tissue to wipe the orange-coloured spittle dribbling down his chin.

After Kaska has left, Kenny, Philippa and Shogun share a doughnut. It smells delicious but my stomach doesn't rumble even though it's empty, haha.

They are watching a programme in which a family is considering moving to Australia. The pretty presenter reminds me of Philippa, despite being probably a few years younger and a few inches shorter, oh, and not as dark haired – but apart from that.

Kenny's dozing. Between dozes Philippa asks him the story of whether or not we were once close to emigrating to Australia. It's an old story and true, but Kenny says, 'Were we? I don't remember.'

Philippa already knows the story. Her half-smile freezes, then collapses into pursed lips. It's so sad that a little more of Kenny's memory has died. With it, a little more of me dies – I didn't know that was possible.

They were hard but good times, just before Philippa was born, in 1960. Kenny was working for London Transport but the work on the lines was physical and the pay wasn't great. I was trying to be a better seamstress at a small clothing factory, making mostly cheap cotton underwear in the days before it was even cheaper to make it abroad and ship it to England – I never understood how that worked, we were already paid so poorly, and the factory was a dangerous slum. But we were getting by, living with my parents though we'd married by then. We had the upstairs, they had the downstairs. Kenny and my dad converted the box room to a small kitchen with a sink we could use for washing, and we used what was the front bedroom as a lounge. Downstairs my parents used the front room as a bedroom and the backroom as their lounge. The toilet was still in the lean-to extension out back, and we had a rota for weekly baths in the tin tub that was brought in from the shed. Me and Kenny shared the hot water, if not the bath. I doubt Dad would approve, even though we were married.

Dad had just bought a second-hand Bush TV – the screen was probably not even a foot and a half across – and some evenings we'd go downstairs to watch with them, but mostly we'd stay upstairs, reading, listening to the radio, doing jigsaws or making a rug for the new house we were saving a deposit for. But it was hard, and the winter was cold. Come December, fed up with scraping ice from the inside of the windows, we were sorely tempted by the adverts of just a tenner for passage to Australia. I like to think we'd have been adventurous enough to go – Kenny was desperate for a new start – but then I fell pregnant with Philippa. My mum insisted she would be all right with not knowing her grandchild, but I was never going to deny her that. We stayed and not once did Kenny hold it against me, even when my mum died just a month before Philippa was born. The cancer that took her was a slow one, but she'd been even slower to go to the doc, so it all felt very quick to us. My dad sold the house, gave me and Kenny the deposit for our first place, and moved back up to his hometown in Yorkshire. He couldn't abide living in the house he had shared with Mum. So maybe we could have gone to Australia. I think about it now and again but, tell the truth, I don't think it would have made much difference to us. For Philippa? Who knows. She'd never have met Ciaran and might have had children with someone else – maybe. As it happens, I hardly saw my dad again anyway. Living in Australia wouldn't have made that much difference. It's not that he didn't want to be part of our new family, or that we didn't want him to be. It's just that, when Mum died, he sort of gave up and was gone himself in only another year. Though I accept that by walking in front of a bus he had only himself to blame. I don't think about that. Did he mean to? What might he have been thinking at the time? I never think about that. What might he have been feeling? I never dwell on it. I'm not brave enough. And though I think he deserves better from me, I know he would never want me to 'go there'. Kenny spent years telling me I was not to blame, and he was sincere, every time, but not convincing, because I would not let him be, despite agreeing with him, and he knew that but never stopped trying. My God it was, is, complicated.

Anyway, that's the Australia story – not really an Australia story at all – though of course I sometimes wonder what would have happened if we could have taken Dad with us, but he'd never have left the country of Mum's grave, never. And I doubt we'd have been allowed to dig her up and take her – I know, really not funny, but it's better than thinking about Dad and that bus.

So, hard times. Not all sad though. We had Philippa. And after Sasha, she was, of course, everything.

The family on the TV has chosen to move to Australia. Philippa wishes them well and envies them the climate. Kenny mentions in passing that it was, 'Bloody hot in Hong Kong. And wet.'

That's where he served some of his National Service. That much he does remember, bless him, before dozing off again, bless him. Shogun is also now napping, occasionally twitching furiously, and I wonder if he catches the cat in his dreams.

Philippa picks up the sketch of the cat from earlier and, absent-mindedly it seems, adds a few more pencil lines and some shading. Miraculously, a girl appears next to the cat. The girl is wearing a pinafore, similar to Philippa's secondary school uniform, and looks like a friend that came to tea often – I remember, as if yesterday, their laughing and giggling, but the name is forgotten. I bet Philippa remembers. The girl was her best friend for a couple of years. She had many friends, in and out of school. Where have they all gone? I think back to those trips to the park when I sat and watched her play. I wasn't good at chatting with the other mums, but luckily Philippa didn't need me to teach her how to mix.

Rebecca. The name of the other girl comes to me. Rebecca. I wonder what happened to Rebecca. I think she was one of Philippa's bridesmaids. I remember the night Ciaran asked her to marry him. She had taken well to the art classes and arranged the annual show at the community centre. We were so proud that night. Ciaran was so proud. Her watercolour of our local church won third prize – and easily deserved first, but then as she had organised the show that might have looked suspicious. We went down the pub afterwards. Ciaran took Kenny to one side for a chat and I wondered what was going on. When they came back to our table, Ciaran went down on bended knee and asked Philippa to marry him. He must have been sure of the answer to ask in such a public place.

I look again at the newly sketched figure next to the scary cat – yep, that's Rebecca.

Kenny stirs and farts loudly and, I fear, wetly. Philippa sighs and starts for the bedroom and the hoist. Shogun follows, woken by the fart perhaps and hopeful of a treat, of course. But before Philippa can bring the hoist through there is a solid knock at the door. Philippa grabs the barking dog by the collar and opens the door to Lewis. He's red in the face, it's still a warm day, and the top button of his shirt is undone, the silk tie's Windsor knot dropped an inch, but he smiles broadly.

'Here for Shogun. Thank you so much for rescuing

him from that cat,' Lewis jokes and it's quite funny, if hard to hear over Shogun's ecstatic barking. Lewis looks down at Philippa. She's bent over, holding Shogun's collar – he's a much smaller dog than he himself realises – and I think I catch Lewis glancing at the gaping top of Philippa's dress. And why not? She has a fine bosom, perkier than mine, haha. Lewis focuses on Philippa's face as she lets Shogun free, but I wonder if she also noticed his furtive peek as she holds herself tall and straightens her dress.

'How did the interview go?' she asks.

'Good thanks. Better than good. They offered me the job.' Lewis has picked up Shogun and holds him at arm's length. The dog strains to lick his master's face.

'Congratulations.' Philippa is genuine.

'Thank you. I start in a fortnight.'

'Nice to get some good news. Will you celebrate later?'

'Well, now that you mention it, I did wonder if, not tonight, but maybe Friday evening, we might go for a drink? Perhaps The White Hart?' Lewis's already red face turns a shade darker and he relents to let Shogun take a lick.

Philippa hesitates – my silent prompting remains, obviously, silent – then stumbles over a few words,

'That's a nice … thought, idea … and … good to celebrate good news … it's just that, well, I've got a works do, ex-works really, I don't work there anymore, this Friday. It's an annual summer thing.'

I look at Philippa. Lewis takes a half step back. Neither of us was expecting this. The last I saw, the ex-works do invite was stashed in the 'get to eventually' pile next to the unused coffee percolator.

'Oh,' says Lewis, disappointed. 'Of course, no problem.' He nods, for some reason, and I think he's about to leave when he asks, 'How about Friday week then?' He has a nice smile and a full set of teeth.

Philippa hesitates, she didn't count on this. Shogun looks at her, expecting an answer.

'That sounds ok … yes, why not. I just need to check

the date. But it would make a nice change. I'll need to find someone to sit with Dad, you know, what with his … you know.'

'Of course, and if you like I can ask Mum. I'm sure she won't mind.'

Philippa frowns and I hope she feels my reticence. I don't want Joyce in here, looking after Kenny; judging.

'Hold off asking Joyce,' says Philippa. 'Let me check the date, just in case, and get back to you, in a day or two.'

'Of course, just let me know. And thanks again for …' he holds up Shogun like a trophy.

Chapter 7

Wednesday 26th June
Kiss Me Goodnight Sergeant Major

Two days after that first respite 'experiment', Kaska returns. Kenny's finishing breakfast, Philippa's apologising for being, 'all behind'. Kaska assures her, sincerely, that it doesn't matter. The OH man had rung on the evening of Kaska's first visit, wanting to know how it had gone, and Philippa agreed it was all right and the Wednesday booking could go ahead. She was a little reticent, partly, I think, due to pride, partly because, although Kaska seemed lovely, she's still a stranger, and partly because of the money. I can't hear the other side of the conversation but the OH man must have been gently persuasive. Philippa's not one to be brow-beaten but is smart enough to listen to reason, and I like to think me and Kenny had something to do with that. She has never been unnecessarily stubborn, unlike Kenny, occasionally, bless him. But, whatever, the cost will be playing on her mind. She has been joking to Kenny that she may have to go and get a job. Kenny thinks it's a good idea. I tell her she should try selling some of her artwork but she's stubbornly ignoring me.

So, Kaska is back on Wednesday. The four of us are in the kitchen, they are sitting round the table, chatting easily. Or rather, Philippa and Kaska are. Kenny is rearranging coasters and placemats.

'A lovely day. Are you going to the shops?' Kaska asks.

'To the park, to read.' Philippa taps the paperback in front of her. The bookmark is in the same place as when she brought it back on Monday.

Philippa makes herself a flask of coffee. Kaska assures her Kenny will be fine. Kenny looks up from his task and asks Kaska, 'Who are you?'

Kaska laughs, 'Kaska, of course.'

Kenny smiles. 'Of course.'

Philippa returns a little before the hour is up. I notice the bookmark has moved on and the flask is empty. Philippa's cheeks are a little rosy – fresh air and sunshine. Kaska gives Philippa a handover report in clear, definitive terms. Kenny's now sitting in his riser/recliner watching a YouTube video of cartoonishly cute puppies stumbling across a lawn. TVs are clever these days, aren't they? Kenny and mine's first one was a Philips, from Radio Rentals. He nearly fell off the roof trying to tune the bloody thing; him up on the tiles twisting the aerial slowly; me downstairs shouting up when the signal was clearest.

Philippa and Kaska join Kenny in the lounge.

'Hello, I know you,' Kenny says to Philippa, and tells Kaska, 'This is my wife.'

'Not wife, Dad, daughter,' says Philippa, forcing a smile. 'And who's this?' Philippa asks Kenny, indicating Kaska.

Kenny smiles at her. 'You're … you're my friend.'

'Yes, I am Kaska.'

Kenny copies her, 'Kaska,' adding, 'That's a funny name.'

'Thank you for sitting with him,' Philippa says to Kaska as she walks to the door. 'Say goodbye, Dad.'

But instead Kenny says, 'She does talk funny, doesn't she?'

Kaska hears. This time she returns to the room, kneels down at Kenny's side and takes his hand. 'Yes, I do. But that doesn't matter, does it Kenny? Actually, it's a good thing, don't you think? I do. We are all God's creatures, aren't we? I am Polish.' She smiles at Kenny who smiles back and nods.

Philippa stands awkwardly to one side, not knowing what to do.

'Polish? I served with a few,' says Kenny, 'not National Service, like me, but regulars, still there after the war. Good men, always joking. I liked them. Good with motors too.' He looks past Kaska to the garden but his stare is back to some memory.

Philippa's trying to look apologetic on behalf of Kenny. 'I doubt Kaska has been in the army, Dad.'

'Actually, I was conscripted when I was twenty. It was necessary in my country to serve. So you see, Sergeant Kenny, we are comrades in arms.' She salutes and now I fancy I see a memory stirring in Kaska's face.

She pecks him on the cheek. Kenny beams and starts to sing, 'Kiss me goodnight Sergeant Major, tuck me in my little wooden bed ...' but the song falls away as the words fail him. Then he says, 'Those Poles. Good men. Talked funny though. Foreign like.'

Philippa takes a breath and leads Kaska away from Kenny. 'I'm sorry. I'll talk to him. He can be ... insensitive.' I'm glad that Philippa doesn't try to pretend it wasn't said or means nothing.

'Thank you,' says Kaska, knowing it won't make much difference. I expect she has seen and heard this all before, but they both know that doesn't make it ok. The atmosphere is a little awkward.

'Out of interest,' Philippa asks hesitantly, 'do you sit with people in the evenings? Private work I mean, not through Social Services. I would pay you, of course.'

'Sometimes. For the right client,' Kaska teases.

'It's just. Well, I'm meant to be going to a do this Friday and I wasn't going to, but then I told someone I would, so I suppose I should. But I can't leave Dad.'

'What is a do?'

'A party. More of a casual get together really. Nothing special at all. Just a drink with some old workmates.'

Behind them Kenny starts to sing again, 'Kiss me goodnight Sergeant Major ...' but again the words fall away. Kaska looks over her shoulder,

'Of course. Fifteen pounds an hour. But for Kenny, twelve. What time?'

The Michaelmas Daisy

Chapter 8
Friday 28ᵗʰ June
Pippa

Twelve pounds an hour to sit with Kenny. I know I'm dead but my hearing is all right, so did Kaska really mean twelve an hour? And that's the private, cash in hand rate. How much is Philippa – Kenny – paying Social Services for the respite hours during the day? I don't think she's paying full whack, but even so.

After Philippa was born I didn't work until she started primary school, and even then it was part-time. It was all right for her to walk to school in the mornings with friends, but I always tried to be home when she walked in the door. There were a lot of latchkey kids down our street, but no way was Philippa going to be one of them, so I was usually home before her, though she did have a key – sometimes I had to work late for a few extra bob. Jobs like part-time cigarette packer – not by hand, there was a machine, obviously, I've not been dead that long – didn't pay twelve quid a week; nowhere near, probably not even half that. Some of the girls nicked a few packs every week to sell on but I never did – too scared of being caught, like Eileen who was sacked for less than forty fags and threatened with a police caution, though I'm pretty sure our local copper, we called him Whistler, wouldn't have taken it that far. He was a good man, a reasonable man, had a sense of justice and was very persuasive. He once stopped Kenny on his motorbike when he was riding home from work – it was the wobbling that caught his eye, he knew Kenny to be a good rider. Anyway, Kenny had a load of copper wire in one of the saddlebags, weighing a ton, unbalancing the bike. Whistler found it, of course, and knew it had to be dodgy, but just suggested to Kenny that no more find its way into Kenny's bag, and what was there should find its way back to where it came from – and that was the end of the matter.

He was great at showing the kids across the main road to school in the morning too.

Anyway, I was usually home for Philippa after school and that was important to Kenny. He was a provider and a grafter. My God, he was a grafter.

He worked long hours, and not just on the railways. At home he built the extension by hand, from scratch. He rewired upstairs, crazy-paved the drive, put up a shed, re-fenced the garden – watched closely by Blofeld, who immediately peed on the new posts to christen them – fixed the telly when a valve blew, and replastered the lounge ceiling. Together we hung wallpaper, painted doors, skirtings and architraves, finished making that rug and were a great team in the garden. We dug a vegetable patch – times were hard, Kenny packed up smoking to save money, but he loved rhubarb; I never told him Blofeld peed on that too – planted shrubs and beds and laid a patio with a veranda style roof. I was a grafter too.

I look over at Philippa, putting Kenny to bed. It's only half past six but she wants him settled before Kaska arrives, and she needs to give herself time to get ready for the ex-works do tonight.

Kenny's suspended in the hoist. Philippa pulls up his clean incontinence pants and pyjama trousers then manhandles the hoist into place to lower him on to the bed. He relaxes as he feels his bottom reach the mattress. Philippa unstraps him and hauls the machine back into the corner. She dresses Kenny in a clean vest and pyjama top – the buttons are fiddly – then lifts Kenny's legs while simultaneously lowering his back down to the mattress and spinning him through ninety degrees so he can lie down – this is no mean feat. She tucks him in – light blankets, it's a warm evening – and turns on the TV that sits on my dressing table. She finds a documentary about trains, thanks to Freeview, and passes Kenny the remote control. There was a time he'd happily flick through channels but now he looks at the remote, confused. Philippa puts it back on the dressing table, next to the old photo album, and lifts the bed rails into place, making sure they are properly secured. She puts her hand to Kenny's mouth and asks for his teeth. He pushes them out with his tongue and she puts them in the glass on the bedside table, next to the Tommee Tippee cup. She tells Kenny she'll be back in a minute. On the way out she catches sight of herself in my dressing table mirror and takes a second to brush at the darkening rings under her eyes. The shading doesn't go away. She's tired. She's halfway out the door when she remembers the teeth and returns for the glass. It needs a denture cleaning tablet and water.

Putting Kenny to bed early meant an earlier dinner and toileting, and there's still the kitchen to tidy and the washing-up to do. I told Kenny years ago we should get a dish washer but he wouldn't hear of it. Philippa sorts out the denture glass and the kitchen, and runs the Hoover round the lounge where Kenny dropped a cracker.

She's a grafter.

When she first moved in with Kenny, not long after I died and her divorce from Ciaran, she went back to the art classes and even taught there to earn a little extra cash – money's always tight. But when Kenny could no longer be left alone she gave that up. I think she misses it. I miss that she no longer makes as much time to draw or paint. I so loved watching her at peace.

Finally, she takes a minute, sitting at the kitchen table. But only a minute. It's nearly seven. She has to be at the 'do' by eight and Kaska will be here in half an hour.

'Private Kaska reporting for duty!' Kaska salutes as she enters Kenny's bedroom. He looks up from the covers around him that he has been trying to flatten, and over Kaska's shoulder to Philippa, standing at the door. Philippa nods and Kenny salutes Kaska back.

'I'll just be a minute,' Philippa tells them and goes back upstairs to finish getting ready. It's half past seven. Kaska is bang on time.

I stay with Kenny and Kaska. She wears a light cotton frock, emerald-green with a print of large white flowers. The dress matches her eyes – the green that is, not the flowers, haha. Her blonde hair is short, but not quite boyish, and I wonder again how old she is. She looks younger than she is, I'm sure; petite, full of energy but somehow 'knowing' – I think she's been around a bit, in a good way. She passes Kenny the Tommee Tippee cup, encouraging him to drink. He coughs at the first sip, as usual, and Kaska frowns, dabbing his mouth with a tissue.

Kaska pulls a chair next to the bed and sits. 'So, Sergeant Kenny … What are we watching?'

'Never a Sergeant. Just a common MO.'

'MO? What is that?'

Kenny, thoughtful, looks at her, then laughs. 'I don't know.'

'And I don't. But that's ok.' Kaska laughs with him and starts singing, 'Kiss me goodnight Sergeant Major, tuck me …'

Kenny joins in,

'… in my little wooden bed.'

… and Kaska goes on to sing the first verse and chorus. She has taken time to learn the song. Kenny knows the tune and the words come to him, a second after Kaska sings them, but they come to him. When the song finishes, they sing it again – I like Kaska — then watch the trains on TV, and I think Kenny's often close to saying something but never quite finds the words. To be fair, he was never big on chit-chat. Not that he was curt or rude, but he liked to get to the point. These days, it's hard for him to find it. When Philippa first began looking after him she would try to help him get to the point, but has learnt that it's not important anymore; it doesn't help Kenny to try and find it. It didn't help Philippa either.

'So, Sergeant Kenny … What did you do in the army?' asks Kaska.

'MO.'

'What does that mean?'

'Medical Orderly.'

Now it comes to him.

'Like a doctor?'

Kenny looks at her, confused. 'Do you?'

Kaska chuckles. 'In the army, I was a driver. Big trucks.' She mimes holding a steering wheel and bounces on the chair.

'They let you drive?'

'Of course.'

'But you're tiny.' Kenny calls it as he sees it.

I remember him telling me the same when I asked him to teach me to ride his Thunderbird. He was adamant I wasn't big enough to hold the weight at rest. Turned out he was right. I fell off at the top of the road. It was the only time I think he had a 'told you so' moment with me, through gritted teeth. After that we got a second-hand Morris Traveller. He taught me to drive in that. I only scraped it a couple of times. In truth, I rarely drove even after I'd passed; usually when Kenny was tipsy. We brought Philippa home from hospital in that car. No seat belts or baby seat. I sat in the back and held her on my lap.

Ciaran tried teaching Philippa to drive, soon after they got engaged, in his Ford Escort. It was going ok until he asked her to reverse up the drive. He was behind, giving directions and didn't move fast enough when she hit the accelerator instead of the brake. She nearly killed him – oh the irony of a nurse having to visit A&E. His fellow nurses laughed. Kenny laughed. Eventually, so did Ciaran.

Philippa comes in. Her long hair is tied into a ponytail – I never thought that look suited her, though she said Ciaran liked it. But is it a look for a fifty-nine-year old greying woman? She wears a fitted, navy skirt and light blue blouse. Her shoes have kitten heels – with her height she doesn't need more – and she carries a small clutch bag. She wears her bright red silk Hermes shawl. I brought that home for her from Paris – my first trip abroad in 1985. Her make-up is nicely understated, she has good teeth, sparkling eyes and only a couple of small liver spots on her clear skin which could easily be taken for freckles. I think she looks lovely. I wonder what I look like these days. Mirrors show nothing, but maybe that's for the best. In my mind I'm back to twenty years old, trim and wearing a dark blue dirndl skirt, tight at the waist, full in the skirt, and a white jersey cotton cardigan. My hair is quite short, part permed on top. I wear little make-up, Kenny's not one for, 'painted ladies,' but he does like me to keep my eyebrows neat. They are, oddly, so much darker than my auburn hair. My hair wasn't often long enough for a ponytail; perhaps that's why I don't like Philippa's.

Philippa kisses Kenny on the cheek.

'You're my …' Kenny falters but smiles, happy to see Philippa. 'I know you.'

Kaska stands to greet Philippa and nods approvingly. 'You look very nice. This … do … is a little … posh, I can see.' She indicates to the Hermes scarf. I think she recognises the brand.

Philippa frowns. 'Well, I wouldn't call it posh. It's just a get together, ex-workmates, in the old canteen. I won't even be drinking.' She mimes driving.

'Well you look very nice. Doesn't she, Kenny?'

'I do know you. You're my daughter,' says Kenny, proud of both Philippa and himself for remembering.

Philippa kisses him on the cheek again, then hesitates before asking, 'Does this look all right, Dad? It's just a works do.'

Kenny looks puzzled but that's ok, it's not really him she's asking.

'You look lovely, truly,' says Kaska, 'but if it's not posh …' Kaska takes the silk shawl from Philippa's shoulders. Philippa tenses slightly at the touch and almost flinches as Kaska ties it around her waist and pulls it tight, gypsy style. It does look both more womanly and girly. 'What do you think now, Kenny?' Kaska asks.

Philippa is quiet, unused to such physical contact with a stranger; unused to any contact at all these days, I suppose. She doesn't know what to say and goes out to the hall to use the mirror there. I go with her and whisper, then shout, that Kaska might be right, as long as it's not a posh do.

Philippa spins and poses in front of the glass before putting the printed silk back to a shawl and returning to the bedroom. 'The do might be a little posh.' Philippa shrugs as if in apology.

Kaska nods.

'Help yourself to tea, coffee, whatever. Kenny will be dropping off soon I expect. I pull the curtains around eight. He won't need the toilet again and he's taken all his tablets. Maybe a cup of tea later and …' Philippa stops, realising it's unnecessary. 'You guys will be fine, I'm sure. You've got my mobile.'

'Of course,' says Kaska.

Kenny doesn't look too sure until Kaska sings, 'Kiss me goodnight …'

… then he joins in, saluting Philippa. Philippa listens to Kaska guiding Kenny through the song and is impressed. 'Thank you for that,' she offers Kaska, sincerely.

Kenny salutes Kaska and asks, 'Who are you?'

'Private Kaska. We are soldiers in arms, MO Kenny!'

I stay with Kenny while Philippa's out. Kaska stays too, until Kenny falls asleep; it's a summer evening and not yet dark, but Kenny's body clock ticks to its own rhythms. Kaska settles in the lounge, popping back to check on Kenny every fifteen or twenty minutes. She refreshes his squash even though it's still half-full. He sleeps fitfully these days, but rarely moves. He shows no sign of dreaming, though surely he is. When I shared a bed with him – and in all those years there were only fifteen nights when we didn't; five when he had his appendix out, seven when I gave birth to Philippa and three when I was kept in after losing Sasha. Fifteen out of thousands, amazing – he dreamed and stirred often, often waking me. Sometimes he had nightmares and I would wake him with a firm prod. He was usually grateful but never told me the nightmare's content when I asked in the morning. Once, panicked, he shouted for his mother. It was the only time I heard him call her name. She died when he was a child and he rarely talked of her; only once or twice did I get a glimpse of how much she was missed. I wonder if he misses her still. I wonder if he remembers her name. I do: Dorothy. I wonder where Dorothy is now? I wonder where all the others are while I am still here. There are so many that could, should, be here too, surely?

I wish Philippa would ask Kenny about Dorothy before it's too late. How sad if I am the only one left who knows her name. How sad if no one else knows how much Kenny loved her and, no doubt, she loved him. How sad if no one knows of Dorothy, the mother.

How sad if there is no one after Philippa who will know how much Kenny and I love each other.

How sad if Philippa hasn't understood how much Kenny and I love her.

Being dead is sad. For us and the living, though they may not know it.

Kaska comes back in, closes the curtains even though it's still not dark, and pulls the covers to Kenny's neck. He wakes and she apologises and, recognising his confusion, explains she is Kaska, Philippa knows she is here and will return soon.

'You're my friend,' says Kenny, though it's more a question than a statement. Kaska agrees and sits next to him, raising the head of the bed so that Kenny is sitting up. She holds the Tommee Tippee cup to his mouth so that the merest amount drips through. Kenny seems to be holding the liquid in his mouth. Kaska catches his gaze and makes a show of swallowing heavily. Kenny copies and doesn't choke.

Pippa

Kaska takes the photo album from the dressing table and lays it on Kenny's lap. It's a heavy book with a thick, dark brown, leather cover, embossed with a dove. Why a dove? I've no idea. I don't know where the album came from but we have had it always. Kaska gently opens the pages. There are black and white polaroids, with white borders, held in place by corner mounts. Between the dry, yellowing pages are sheets of tissue, keeping the pictures separate, safe, special. It smells musty.

Kenny watches as Kaska slowly and carefully rolls through the pages, enthralled by the faces staring back at her – the seriousness, the happiness, the pride, the love; all of life, not dimmed by the lack of colour, and alive with joy, significance and consequence. Kaska asks Kenny for names, but he has forgotten and does not even try to remember. I do, and shout them out, pointlessly. It doesn't matter. Names not known doesn't mean strangers, unfamiliar scenes or feelings not shared and understood – to any onlooker. I don't suppose Kaska has spent time on a deck chair on Brighton prom with her gran or watched a niece or nephew hold a lighted sparkler on Guy Fawkes night, but that doesn't matter – she has lived a version of these photos, I'm sure. We all have. She understands.

These are pictures of here, now and everyone, as much as yesterday and those who have passed.

Kaska finds a picture of our wedding day and tells Kenny how handsome he was, true, and how beautiful I was; also true – the time for modesty is long gone. Kenny smiles and nods. I suspect Kaska has questions to ask about the relatives and friends lined up either side of us but will not cause Kenny any stress by asking. She dwells on the page. Kenny takes over the turning and stops at a posed photo of me, wearing a stunning ball gown that I borrowed for a proper posh do. I don't remember the occasion but I remember the dress – scarlet; shame the picture is not in colour – and I had it for just one night, desperately careful not to spill so much as a drop on it.

'That's my wife,' Kenny tells Kaska.

'Very … elegant. A beauty.' Kaska hesitates. I want her to ask him my name, sure that Kenny will know. But what if he's forgotten? That would be unbearable. I hope she doesn't ask.

'And did she have a charming name?' Kaska asks quietly.

I hold my breath and pray. Kenny half-opens his mouth.

We hear the front door open.

Philippa is home at just gone nine fifty. She has been out barely two and a quarter hours. Kaska checks her watch.

'Did you have a nice time? Was it a good … do?'

'Ok, thanks. All ok here?'

'Of course.' Kaska gives Philippa an update in her more formal tone. I could tell Philippa it's a factual and accurate report. 'Did you leave your scarf there?' Kaska finishes with a question, noticing that Philippa isn't wearing her Hermes shawl.

'Oh, I left it in the car. Turns out it wasn't posh at all. I was a bit … overdressed.' Philippa looks a little embarrassed.

'Overdressed? Does that mean you had too many clothes on? Did the others wear swimsuits?' Kaska laughs.

'Not quite but …'

'There's my Pippa.' Kenny calls out, interrupting. He rests a finger on a photo in the album.

My heart leaps then is crushed.

Pippa.

Kenny's pet name for Philippa. His girl.

Pippa.

More than a name. A prayer, a promise. Every time he used that pet name he was telling her how much he loved her, would die for her, would sell his soul for her to be happy and well.

Pippa.

I think Philippa understood all that, from the very first.

Pippa

No one else called her that, not even me. I never begrudged them that. I was never jealous.

And when Philippa was a teenager she pretended it was embarrassing but, truth is, any embarrassment was a small price to pay for that devotion. I don't know if it was ever a burden for her. I hope not. Kenny would be gutted to think so.

Pippa.

The last time I heard Kenny say that name was on the morning of her wedding.

'There's my Pippa.' Kenny repeats himself.

Philippa and Kaska look at the photograph.

Kenny and Philippa – Pippa – are in the garden. Philippa is on her first bike. Kenny's holding the saddle to keep the bike upright as he smiles at the camera. Philippa's face is a study in concentration. I remember that day. Boxing Day. It was a cold hour in the garden. Philippa on the bike, Kenny running alongside, up and down the path, holding the saddle until no longer needed. Philippa so serious until her dad could let go.

'Pippa?' Philippa whispers. I think maybe she had forgotten, until now. She looks at Kenny.

'You're my Pippa,' says Kenny, smiling.

My heart bleeds for them. My heart bleeds for me.

Philippa blinks away a tear, gulps a breath, and holds it for a few seconds before whispering, 'Of course, Dad.'

I wonder, if Sasha had lived, would Kenny have given him a pet name? Would I? We had proper names ready: Emily for a girl, Robert for a boy. But he will forever remain a Sasha.

Philippa looks through a few more photos with Kenny but her thoughts are elsewhere. She persuades Kenny to have a sip of orange squash then settles him down before joining

Kaska in the kitchen. It's ten past ten. There is a pot of tea stewing on the table next to a colouring book. Kaska is completing a complicated butterfly pattern, careful not to go over the black lines with her felt tip pens. Next to the tea pot is the pad on which Philippa sketched the cat, and her friend, Rebecca. She has added other drawings – some exquisitely detailed flowers, a rough outline of Palma Cathedral, the start of a dog that might become Shogun. Kaska puts down the deep purple and looks up as Philippa sits down. Philippa's eyes are wet but she won't let tears fall.

'Pippa is a nice name,' says Kaska.

'It was, a long time ago.'

'I have not heard it before.'

'It was his pet name for me.'

Kaska looks confused and Philippa explains about pet names.

'Does it have a meaning?'

'No, just a way to shorten Philippa.'

'Ah, my father called me Kotku.'

'Does that mean something?'

'You would say little cat or kitty.'

'Ah, Kotku Kaska. That's nice. Does he still call you that?'

'He stopped calling me that a long, long time ago. Kenny doesn't call you Pippa anymore?'

Philippa pours tea, hesitating over the answer. 'No, I can't remember the last time. I thought we had both forgotten.' Her eyes dampen more.

I remember the last time – that morning of her wedding. He had it in mind, foolishly, that when Philippa married Ciaran she'd not be his Pippa anymore. We were in the lounge, waiting for the cars to take us to church. Philippa came in, looking beyond radiant – my heart ached to see such beauty. We were so proud. Kenny wanted to cry but never had in front of Philippa and wouldn't now. He took her hand and said simply, 'You're Ciaran's Pippa now, but I'll always be your dad.'

How is it Philippa doesn't remember that? Though looking at the effort needed to still her tears I think perhaps she does.

'Do you remember the last time your father called you Kotku?'

Kaska drops a sweetener into her cup. 'Not really. He died,' she does some mental maths, 'seven years ago, but he stopped calling me that long before then, when I asked if I could bring home a girlfriend. I was nearly twenty-two, so, seventeen years ago.'

'He didn't want you to bring home a friend?'

Kaska thinks for a second before replying. 'She was a close, very close, girl … friend. He was … Polish, Catholic and old-fashioned.' She forces a laugh.

Philippa and I take a couple of seconds for the implication to register.

'I'm sorry,' says Philippa.

I don't think I've ever knowingly met a gay lady before – or gay man for that matter, though there were rumours about Brian who ran the HR department at the cigarette factory. And then there was Philippa's first teacher at primary school – Miss Nachem. She always wore slacks and had a deep voice, so the school-gate mums talked about her, but she was very pretty. Then again so is Kaska. I want Philippa to ask Kaska when she realised she was gay, how her mother reacted, what her other friends thought, how she met other gay ladies, how they … you know; though I appreciate that would be a question too far, even for me. But Philippa is quiet.

Kaska fills the silence before it's awkward. 'I came to England a year later. I didn't … don't, go back often.'

Now I want Philippa to ask if Kaska's mother is still alive, does she have brothers and sisters, how did her father die?

It's not for idle gossip. I just don't get out much – haha – so any interesting details about others' lives are, well, interesting. Especially if it's a gay lady. When I was growing up we didn't know of any gay ladies, though there were a few couples, both women, that not only lived together but, now I think of it, were close and shared lives; especially after the war. I don't remember anyone making anything of it; perhaps because it was after the war.

'Anyway, Kotku never really suited. Fathers can expect too much sometimes,' says Kaska.

Philippa nods but, to be fair, Kenny was never like that, I don't think. Perhaps Philippa thinks different?

Kaska checks her watch, changes the subject, 'You came home early?'

Philippa smiles half-heartedly. 'I didn't want it to be a late night for you.'

'It's ok, I don't work tomorrow until the evening. You could have stayed out. I'm not your father.' Kaska laughs. So does Philippa.

'Actually, I didn't know as many people there as I thought I might. It's been a while since I left and there seems to be fewer and fewer of my old colleagues. It was good to catch up with those that I used to work with. I miss them, but then I got caught by Hamish.'

'Hamish?'

'Oddly, he's French rather than Scottish.'

Kaska's confusion isn't helped by that explanation.

'He was mansplaining how latest gen CAD and open source programming is going to revolutionise tech-drawing.'

'Of course,' says Kaska.

'I wouldn't mind,' adds Philippa, 'but I remember proper old, old-school tech drawing, before any CAD at all. Paper, pens, rulers and drawing boards.'

'Hamish, mansplaining, CAD, tech-drawing. I do not understand. Was it not an English do?' asks Kaska.

Philippa smiles, 'It might as well not have been. That's draughtsmen and engineers for you.'

'And you didn't go with a man friend or meet one there?'

Philippa is a little taken aback by the sudden frankness. Kaska's smile is one of encouragement.

Philippa pauses and considers her answer. 'I don't have a man friend. I haven't had one since I divorced. It's difficult. I don't get out much.'

Kaska pauses, thinking – I think she changes her mind – then asks, 'Yours?' indicating to the sketches.

Philippa nods.

'The same cathedral as over the fireplace?' She motions to the lounge where Palma Cathedral sits proudly over the mantelpiece.

'It's where I spent my honeymoon. Long time ago.'

'You're very good. I mean, I don't know about art, but it looks good to me.'

'Thank you.' Philippa reddens slightly.

'I have been there. Not for a honeymoon though.'

'Ciaran, my ex, wanted to see it. It is a beautiful place. We stayed in Palma.'

'How long have you been divorced?' It's another personal question but Kaska has a way of asking lightly.

'Oh, eight years.' Philippa looks down into her tea.

'And no man since then?' Kaska smiles cheekily.

'I don't get out much,' Philippa repeats, smiling.

'You should. You're pretty and kind. He would be lucky.'

Philippa blushes, 'Who would?'

'Any man. But I know what you mean. It is difficult. Both the walking away and starting again.'

There is a sadness in Kaska's eyes which she quickly dispels, picking up her phone. 'I might try online next. You could too.'

'Ah, I don't think so.'

'Why not?' Kaska is disarmingly, charmingly, direct.

Philippa frowns. I see she's searching for an answer. 'Actually, I have been asked out recently, by Lewis, from next door. To celebrate his new job.' She points in the direction of Joyce and Lewis's house.

'Ah, the man with the dog? He seems all right. Most men with a dog are. Though it is a stupid dog.'

Philippa laughs.

'Where will he take you?' Kaska asks.

'I haven't said yes yet.'

'But you will. You must. Don't worry, I'll sit with Kenny again. For only ten pounds an hour this time.'

Chapter 9
Saturday 29th June to Friday 5th July
Pain au Chocolat

Saturday: Lewis knocks. He's popping to the shops and asks if we need anything. We … haha. But, as it happens, there is something I want. It's been years, perhaps ten, since I've had a pain au chocolat. Before I fell ill, Kenny and I would walk up to the High Street on a Saturday and treat ourselves from the bakery; hot sausage roll for him, pain au chocolat for me. I'd become a fan back in 1985, during our first holiday abroad, that trip to France. Kenny wanted to go to Spain, but I'd been told – down the salon – it was a bit tacky these days. This was going to be my first trip overseas – I know, I was already fifty – and I wasn't going to be accused of going cheap, especially by Pat The Perm. So we ended up in Paris. We spent a week there – Eiffel Tower, Notre Dame, Arc de Triomphe, Le Louvre; le lot, haha. The Mona Lisa was disappointing – too small, I thought. To tell the truth most of it was; disappointing I mean, not small. The weather was poor, the food was all right, I suppose, but the service was no better than our local Wimpy, and far less friendly. The highlights were flying – my first time; all the hanging around and queuing in the airport was worth it – and buying two Hermes shawls; one in bright red for Philippa and another in forest green for me. They were expensive but it was the year of our thirtieth anniversary. Oh, and another highlight was discovering pain au chocolat.

I know – suppose – that, being dead, I should miss more stuff, and of course I do, like talking and listening – the talking more, I can still listen – cuddling, touching – touching anything, absolutely anything, and I don't mean in a saucy way, just the feel of a soft wool scarf on my cheek would be something, a drop of cold rain on my face would be electric, I'm sure – dressing up, tasting – I can smell but it's not the same – choosing what to watch on TV and which radio station to listen to – I didn't know Philippa was such a fan of classical music. Bach, Mozart, Elgin? What's wrong with Nat, Cliff, Dusty or Andy Williams?

But sometimes it just comes down to a pain au chocolat.

Anyway, Lewis offers to pick up shopping but Philippa says not to worry, she'd done a shop during the week and blah, blah, blah … when all three of us know that Lewis is after an answer to his invite. Lewis waits patiently for her to finish before asking, 'By the way, did you think about that drink?'

Philippa's smile freezes and eventually – it wasn't really long but felt that way to all three of us, I'm sure – says, 'I just need to sort out a sitter for Dad.'

Vague though it is, Lewis seems happy enough with this – perhaps he's forgotten we've been here before. I'm beginning to think he may not be as bright as I first hoped. He waves from the gate. Philippa waves back, closes the door and goes to fill a bowl of hot water to take to Kenny's bedroom. He isn't up yet and the morning routine is about to begin. Philippa takes a sip from her coffee on the way back to the bedroom, grabs a pair of disposable gloves, flannel, and one of the aprons she had delivered a few days ago. These are becoming more necessary as the weeks go by.

Monday: Kaska knocks hard, she knows that if Philippa's busy, and of course she will be, she may not hear a more gentle rap.

'How's Kenny?' she asks as she enters, quickly followed by, 'How are you?'

Philippa is vague on both counts – they are both, 'Well.'

Kaska goes through to the lounge. Kenny's sleeping in his riser/recliner, more recliner than riser at the moment. There is a YouTube video on the TV. Philippa's getting to grips with just how 'smart' this TV can be. Tom Jones is belting out 'Delilah', or at least he would be if the sound was turned up. Philippa presses pause, explaining to Kaska that Tom Jones is a favourite of Kenny's.

'It is a beautiful day. Park again?' asks Kaska.

Philippa opens her tote bag to show the paperback and already prepared flask. She's ready to go.

'Why not take these?' Kaska takes the sketch pad and pencil from the coffee table. 'Pretty goose.'

There is a new sketch on a fresh page, coming along nicely: a swan on calm waters. Philippa hesitates, shrugs and puts it into her bag. 'It's meant to be a swan.'

'Really? Looks like a goose,' Kaska laughs, 'and I grew up on a farm.' She walks with Philippa to the front, telling her, 'I saw the man next door when I arrived.'

'Lewis?'

'Lewis,' agrees Kaska. 'He was just getting into his Mercedes. He smiled at me. Seems nice enough.'

'I guess.' Philippa is wary.

'With a Mercedes,' adds Kaska laughing.

'Does that help?' teases Philippa.

'It doesn't hurt. See you in an hour. No need to rush back, my next job isn't until two.'

Kaska closes the door behind Philippa. It's just the three of us. We go back into the lounge together. I thought she was wearing a maroon, calf-length skirt at first, but now I see they are culottes. She wears a pale-yellow blouse, long sleeved, and a pair of white trainers that look too big for her small feet. Her clothes are also a little big for her, but then she's so petite that perhaps it's inevitable. The effect is to make her almost childlike in appearance apart from her face – the short blonde hair and high cheek bones do not disguise the frown and laughter lines, and though her eyes are a beautiful green, today they are tired. I notice the wrinkles on the back of her hands; hands which have seen much manual labour and water, I'm guessing. I still don't know how old she is but today revise my estimate upwards a little – perhaps late thirties?

Kenny snores. Kaska tucks the light blanket a little tighter around him – it's a warm summer day and the patio doors are open but a breeze slips in. I occasionally hear Shogun bark or a shout from the school. We used to hear a lot of birdsong, but not so much these days. I wonder if that's because Kenny no longer keeps the cats away with his water pistol. I turn to ask him, then catch myself. I pretend it's because I don't want to wake him.

Kaska takes Kenny's Tommee Tippee cup to the kitchen to make him a fresh drink. From her bag she takes a homemade loaf of bread, baked that morning, I guess by the smell. She cuts off a couple of slices, finds the butter in the fridge, and layers on a thick coating. This seems to me to be a bit of a liberty, but she takes the plate into the lounge and sits by Kenny, waiting for him to wake up. She scrolls through her phone then goes back to her bag to bring in a small notebook, colouring book and some pens. She checks the TV and writes 'Tom Jones, 'Delilah',' in the notebook under the heading 'Kenny'. This new entry sits just below 'Kiss Me Goodnight Sergeant Major' in a list – I like Kaska more every time we meet. She takes a look around the room, double checking the picture above the mantelpiece. She turns as if to say something to Kenny – I'm not the only one – but he's still sleeping. She takes the colouring book, chooses a new pattern and settles down to carefully colour the complicated swirls – a strange way for a grown woman to pass the time. I wish I could have a go.

Kaska's concentration is interrupted when Kenny stirs then wakes. He looks around the room then settles on Kaska. 'Do I know you?' His smile is false.

'Of course. I am Private Kaska remember?' She salutes.

Kenny doesn't remember and returns the salute half-heartedly.

'Pippa will be back soon,' says Kaska.

'Pippa?'

'Your daughter,' explains Kaska and points to the

wedding photo of Philippa and Ciaran.

'Pippa?' repeats Kenny.

'Philippa,' Kaska clarifies.

Kenny nods but I suspect it's just to satisfy Kaska, who has put down her colouring and passes him the Tommee Tippee cup. She dispenses a few small sips and tells him, 'Well done,' when he swallows. She suggests some of her fresh bread and butter but he's not hungry.

'And how are you feeling today, Kenny?' asks Kaska.

With no hesitation he says, 'Holding the rails.'

'Good,' says Kaska, and starts to sing the Sergeant Major song. Kenny tries to join in but his heart is not in it. He stares at the TV and Tom Jones. 'I know him.'

Kaska presses play and turns up the volume, but it's not until the chorus that Kenny joins in with, 'Delilah,' and, second time around, Kaska.

Kaska plays the song through four times, offering a drink – taken – and piece of bread – refused – between renditions.

Kenny's not himself today. He was never one for dark moods, at least, not often. Occasionally, when he still rode a motorbike, he would take off on a Sunday for a couple of hours. I never asked where he went, but he always came back more … settled, if not happier. That was in the years shortly after we were married and then lost Sasha. We didn't talk about Sasha much. To me, he was very quickly a blond toddler, never really a baby, who was tall for his age, with dark eyes and an oval face that creased into a smile whenever we walked into the room. I imagine he had a small mole high up on his left cheek – to be perfect would be unreal – and Sasha was, is, very, very real. Sasha is forever a toddler and forever happy. I wonder where he is. I used to look through *Woman's Own* and *Woman's Realm* for ideas on how to dress him and I even knitted a jumper. It wasn't very good and I never showed Kenny.

After Philippa was born, Kenny rarely took off for a ride. But sometimes it was needed, just as I sometimes went up to the library and sat, not reading the book on my lap, for an hour while Kenny looked after Philippa. Mrs. Grenley, the librarian, didn't mind. Sometimes you just need a break, which is why I'm so grateful to Kaska, singing 'Delilah' in that strange but friendly accent of hers, so Philippa can get out.

Just as Kaska is about to find some more Tom Jones songs on the TV YouTube, we both smell Kenny's need to be changed. Again? Was that chicken korma ready meal last night a good idea? Philippa will be back in ten or so minutes but it seems Kaska is determined to complete cleaning Kenny before then. Though small, she drags the hoist into the lounge, gathers the gloves, wipes, eco bin bag and clean pants needed for the job, brings in the commode and swiftly but precisely takes – and talks – Kenny through the routine. He is embarrassed, asking, 'Who are you?' as the sling begins to tension. As usual, he catches a breath when the lift begins and again when his bottom touches the cold plastic of the commode.

Toileting is finished, the commode cleaned, the paraphernalia cleared, and Kenny back in his chair by the time Philippa returns, five minutes late.

Kaska is a grafter.

'I know you. You're my daughter,' says Kenny.

Philippa pecks him on the cheek, 'Holding the rails?'

'Just about,' Kenny smiles.

Kaska gives Philippa a formal update on Kenny while Philippa makes a cup of tea. Kaska has one too – she has time before her next job – and they sit in the lounge, watching Kenny watch Tom Jones, who is now singing 'It's Not Unusual'.

Philippa reaches for her bag and brings out the sketch pad. 'By the way, it's definitely a swan. I went to the pond in the park. They have swans.' Philippa shows Kaska the enhanced sketch.

'Are you sure? It looks much like the geese we had on our farm.' Kaska laughs. 'I wish I could draw. You're very good.' She indicates to Palma Cathedral on the mantelpiece.

Philippa acknowledges, a little embarrassed, and they chat about the cathedral and the city. Kaska spent some months travelling around Europe for work, and she wants to get back to Palma one day. 'Perhaps for my own honeymoon,' she jokes. 'And this is your husband?' She picks up the wedding photo.

'Was,' Philippa acknowledges.

'Good looking,' says Kaska. 'What happened?' Direct questioning as ever.

I pay attention, hopeful of learning something. Philippa shrugs, 'We ... we just drifted apart.'

'Really? That's sad. And since then no one?'

'No.'

'Which is why you must tell the man next door that you'll let him take you out to dinner. I can sit with Kenny.' She leans forward to rest a hand on Philippa's arm. 'Life is short.'

I nod. No one knows that better than me.

'Maybe.' Philippa hesitates, then, 'You grew up on a farm?' Classic Philippa deflection.

'For a few years. It wasn't our farm, my father and mother rented it, but in the end it was too much for them, especially after I left.'

'Was that when you travelled around Europe?'

'Ended up in Worthing. I liked it, my girlfriend didn't. She dumped me.'

'Oh, I'm sorry.'

'Don't be. She slept with a Norwegian barman with an enormous penis and decided she wasn't gay anymore.'

This makes me laugh, after the initial shock at the 'P' word. I can see Philippa doesn't know how to react. Kaska waits a few seconds before laughing. 'Not really. We just, as you say, drifted apart. And she didn't like my cooking.'

'My ex didn't like mine either,' says Philippa.

'I haven't got any better. I've been told.' Kaska is suddenly serious.

'Nor me.' Philippa chuckles, hoping to lighten the moment.

I'm not surprised, about the cooking, that is – since living here to look after Kenny, Philippa's hardly cooked a meal from scratch for either of them. But then I don't blame her, she has more than enough on her plate.

'I am reminded. Kenny hasn't eaten anything while you were out,' says Kaska, 'not even the bread I brought.'

Philippa can smell it. 'Home-made?'

'My … flat mate has a bread machine.'

'Smells lovely.' Philippa nips out to the kitchen, returning with a knife and a pot of jam. 'He has a sweet tooth.' Philippa smears some jam onto the bread, breaks off a small mouthful, with no crust, and shows it to Kenny. He's happy to let her pop it in his mouth.

'My Beverley makes jam,' he tells Kaska, and asks Philippa, 'Where is she?'

And then all hell breaks loose.

In an instant Kenny is gurgling, trying to cough, jerking in the chair, desperate to clear his airways, his frail body wracked with spasms as it fights to both grasp a breath and hack out some blockage. His face is red with panic.

'Dad!' Philippa shouts and pushes up from her chair, tipping over the cup of tea balanced on the arm. 'Dad, Dad!'

I freeze.

Kaska is at Kenny's side a second after Philippa.

Kenny tries to cough harder but fails, he cannot push out air, the blockage is tight. His chest heaves soundlessly, his face is still red and his eyes bulge with fear.

'Dad!' Philippa cries again, kneeling in front of him, shaking.

'Take his arms, pull him forward,' Kaska commands, grabbing the chair's remote control and stabbing at the button to bring it upright. Philippa tugs on Kenny's arms. His convulsions slow.

Kaska tries to force her way behind Kenny, shouting at Philippa to, 'Pull!' until she can just slip her small frame on the chair, wrap her arms around him, make a fist a little below Kenny's rib cage, grab it with her other hand and wrench her arms inwards and upwards in a violent hug.

Philippa hangs on to Kenny's arms, screaming at his now flopping head while Kaska squeezes in sharp, violent spasms. Kenny's body is yanked grotesquely back and forth, a lifeless marionette, his body flapping in Kaska's snatching grasp. On the fifth compression Kenny gags, something has moved. Kaska lets go. Philippa pulls Kenny out of the chair until he's on his knees, then prone on his front. Kaska tumbles from the chair to slap him hard on the back, Kenny's gagging turns to a cough, a wet, clearing hack, and a small piece of bread and jam drops to the floor.

Philippa manages to turn Kenny so he's lying on his side, quietly gasping. Philippa's crying. Kaska is sitting with her knees to her chest, taking deep, calming breaths. I am as still as I ever have been, in life or death, frozen into shock, incapable of thought. Then a burst of energy, from where I know not, surges through me and I am sobbing with anger that I could have been so useless.

Ten minutes later: Kenny is back in his chair. It took both of them and the hoist to lift him from the floor. He's looking out to the garden. That black cat is out there. Where's Shogun when you need him? I try to joke to myself, but it's not funny just now. The room is back to normal apart from the carpet's damp patch of spilled tea near Philippa's armchair. Philippa and Kaska sit in silence, apart from Tom Jones singing 'Green Green Grass Of Home'. Philippa lowers the volume. They sit quietly for another minute. Philippa's flushed, Kaska is pale. She checks her phone,

'I need to go. You ok?' she asks Philippa.

'Of course.'

'You ok, Kenny?' she asks with a salute.

Kenny salutes back, looks at Philippa and says, 'I know

her.'

Philippa walks the hall with Kaska. At the front door, Philippa turns, touches Kaska's arm, and offers, 'Thank you. I don't know what ...' and then heavy tears flow as Philippa tries to apologise.

Kaska's eyes are wet; her turn to apologise, mumbling about the bread being a stupid idea.

Philippa makes a move as if she's going to hug Kaska but stops just short. Both women compose themselves.

'See you Wednesday,' says Kaska as she leaves. 'Oh, and you must tell Lewis about Friday. My price just went down to eight pound an hour. Life is short, no?'

Back in the lounge, Philippa hugs Kenny and asks, 'So, what do you think, Dad? Shall I go out with Lewis?'

He smiles and recites,

'The Michaelmas daisy grows so tall
It sees right over the garden wall,
I wonder, I wonder what it can see
For the Michaelmas daisy is taller than me.'

His favourite ditty, for me and Philippa. He sang it to her when she was a baby and then a toddler, usually when holding and rocking her. He watched her as he sang. She watched him, spellbound.

Kenny said it told of all his hopes and dreams for his Pippa, and was an encouragement that she have her own hopes and dreams beyond our imaginations. I just thought it was an amusing ditty he sang to make me laugh or get back in his good books – which it always did. Perhaps I missed the point.

That evening the OH man rang, checking in to see how it's going with Kaska. I wonder if Kaska has mentioned the choking incident to him. I have a sudden panic that Social Services will take Kenny away, and strain to hear the OH man's side of the conversation, but Philippa is calm and I hear her praising Kaska and agreeing to something. She puts the phone down and tells Kenny,

'Good news, Dad. Social Services have had an update to their budget. They can afford to give us a couple more hours a week of respite time. We'll be seeing more of Kaska. Good, eh?'

Kenny smiles, 'Who's Kaska?'

'Your new friend, Dad.'

'A new friend? That's nice.'

Kenny is happy but I still wonder what Kaska might have told Social Services. It seems co-incidental after today's choking incident. How sad that the only way I feel I can protect them is to be cynical. Being dead is rubbish, but being useless is worse.

Wednesday: Kaska is back. No bread today. Kenny's watching Tom Jones again and Philippa has found a YouTube version of 'Delilah' with subtitles. He can't quite keep up but isn't deterred and enjoys the rhymes in the chorus. I am desperate to put on some Petula Clark but while the TV remote may be within reach, it's a universe away. Philippa and Kaska are chatting in the kitchen about the two extra respite hours and though Kaska can't guarantee it'll be her, she says she'll try. I hope she means it, I think Kenny quite likes her, though he's no idea who she is and her accent is funny.

'And,' she tells Philippa, 'I'll still be ok for some private hours, if you like. Sitting with Kenny in the evening if, you know, you go out with, for example, the neighbour. I'm still free Friday but might have another job lined up soon ...'

Philippa smiles but says nothing.

'You'd be doing me a favour,' adds Kaska. 'I need the money. I have to move out of the flat I'm sharing soon, and need to save a deposit for somewhere new. Ten pound an hour helps ...'

'Wasn't it down to eight?' Philippa asks, laughing.

'Ok. Eight. One time deal if today you tell next door it's ok for Friday. Yes …?'

She lets the thought hang. Philippa doesn't mention that twenty odd quid an evening for a sitter is quite a lot when there's not much coming in. But I hope that won't stop her agreeing.

Philippa doesn't answer.

Philippa returns from the park and unpacks her bag. I notice the bookmark hasn't moved on but the drawing pencil looks a little more blunt. I wonder what she has been drawing – a goose or a swan.

In the lounge, Kenny and Kaska are chanting the tinker, tailor rhyme. It stops with Kaska being 'rich man' when Philippa comes in,

'It means I will have money, soon. So Kenny says.' She shrugs and laughs.

Kenny sees Philippa and holds out a hand. Philippa takes it and kneels at the side of the riser/recliner. 'I know you,' he says.

'And I know you,' says Philippa, pecking him on the cheek.

'And I love you,' says Kenny, and whatever else isn't firing quite right in his brain, there's no doubt he means it more than he ever has in his life. He used to say it to me like that and it was beautiful. Well, not quite like that. There were some subtle colours to it: desire; need; pride; perhaps a touch of fear. To Philippa it's simple, but no less deep and perhaps more pure, beyond doubt.

'And I love you,' says Philippa, grabbing a breath to hold a tear.

Kaska puts the Tommee Tippee cup to Kenny's mouth and he sips. There is a moment of tension and Philippa looks at Kaska, but there's no reason to think there will be a problem. He has eaten and sipped with no problem since choking. Nevertheless, the moment hangs.

On Kenny's lap is the old photo album, open at a picture of a party – Philippa and Ciaran's house-warming. They'd bought a flat when first married and then a house in the late eighties. It was a Victorian two up, two down with a two-storey lean-to extension on the back, and needed lots doing to it. But with Ciaran and Philippa working they had little spare time. So Kenny and I pitched in. It was a tough few months but I wanted the house finished. I thought a finished house meant a nest, meant a grandchild.

They held the party when we'd finished decorating, or, rather, nearly finished. As far as I know the tiny room added at the back upstairs was never properly completed. Perhaps it's just as well – that room was always going to be too cold for a nursery. Besides, it doesn't do to tempt fate. Just before I lost Sasha I'd been re-painting our bedroom – we were still living upstairs at my mum and dad's and I wanted to freshen it up before a baby came, and our bedroom would double as the nursery. I was only undercoating a skirting and a picture rail, but that needed a stepladder. I didn't fall off it, just stumbled on the last step, ending up on my bottom, and the doc was adamant that was not the cause of the miscarriage a week or two later, and Kenny never, not for one second, one instant, thought it my fault, and I honestly don't believe that was the reason we lost Sasha. But still …

Some say that all feelings serve a purpose. Really?

Guilt might be useful *if* you can redeem yourself, but when you can't, it's just inescapable pain.

Guilt might be useful *if* it teaches you not to repeat the cause, but when it can't, it's just gnawing torture.

I've had a long time to think about it, and that's what I say. There is no one to listen.

Anyway, Philippa's was a good house-warming party. I remember it well, despite a few vodka and oranges. Plenty of Ciaran's and Philippa's friends were there and I was dragged – in truth, not much persuasion needed – up to dance to Whitney Houston. She was good, but no Shirley Bassey.

In the picture, Ciaran and Philippa are dancing slowly. They have both turned to look at the camera, and both are smiling naturally. Philippa must have been in heels as she's slightly taller than him; Ciaran would not have minded. They are, to pinch a phrase, a handsome couple. The room is crowded but I can see Kenny sitting in a corner, pint of Guinness in hand. He too is looking at the camera and smiling – I guess it must have been me taking the picture and have no doubt I was smiling back.

Philippa was a great host, engaging her guests, smoothing over the odd drunken argument, proffering nibbles, filling glasses. She used to be confident and good with people.

I think Philippa and Ciaran had good times in that house and I still don't know why they separated.

'Remember that party, Dad?' Philippa asks, pointing to the photo.

'Vaguely,' says Kenny. I suspect he has forgotten, but would rather not admit it.

'Our house-warming,' Philippa tells Kaska.

'Good looking man,' says Kaska, indicating to Ciaran.

'I was,' says Kenny. Philippa and Kaska laugh.

'And you liked a knees up, eh, Dad?'

Kenny bursts in to 'Knees up Mother Brown'. The rest of us join him.

'Ah, so knees up is a party.' Kaska nods. 'Parties are important, need to celebrate when we can. I am good at that. New house, Easter, Christmas, babies … new job.' She looks at Philippa with a wry smile and asks, 'So, Kenny, don't you think Philippa should help your neighbour celebrate his new job?'

Kenny looks at Philippa, unsure if there's a correct answer. Kaska encourages him, 'I don't think Philippa has had a knees up in a while. She should, should she not?'

Kenny nods.

'See,' Kaska tells Philippa.

'I'm not sure,' says Philippa.

'Why would you need to be sure? To be sure would be boring. When I was a teenager I wasn't sure that I wanted to go out with Petr from the next farm. I was right to not be sure. I went to his house, saw his sister and wanted to go out with her instead, but of course I had to go out with Petr at least once.'

'I think you're making my point,' says Philippa, lightly.

'No. If I hadn't agreed to go out with Petr when I wasn't sure, I wouldn't have realised it was his sister I wanted.'

'So say yes to everything then?'

Kaska looks thoughtful. 'Why not?'

'And was it Petr's sister that you travelled Europe with?'

'No, she wasn't gay and didn't like me. But she married my brother, and we had a … good knees up at the wedding, and that's where I met Sophie, so, you see …'

I can see that Philippa doesn't, really, but I think she should say yes to Lewis. If only I could give a signal. There is a vase on the mantelpiece. I try to knock it off, though how that would be a signal I don't know. I wonder if Ouija boards work and how I could get Philippa to try? But what if she did and someone else answered her? That would be terrifying for us all, especially me.

'Eight pounds an hour …' Kaska teases. 'And the Mercedes was outside when I came. I can wait with Kenny while you go next door.'

It's a compelling argument – I think.

It's another ten minutes until Philippa builds the courage, having first changed into a nice summer frock and brushed her hair. Kaska and I watch from the bedroom window. We can see her at Lewis's front door. Philippa hesitates before knocking and, though she's in shadow, I fancy she may be blushing a little. Lewis opens the door and his smile is wide and genuine. There is a brief exchange, they both laugh, there is an awkward pause, then Philippa leaves, talking as she goes. Lewis waits until she's back here before closing the door.

Kaska insists on a full telling of the exchange – the date is 'on' – but cannot stay to hear it as she needs to get to her next job. She says goodbye to Kenny, and Philippa shows her to the front door, saying, '… see you Friday, seven. Have a good afternoon.'

I add, 'Get what you can from it, it won't come round again.'

Friday: Kaska rang earlier to remind Philippa she'd be round at seven, and to offer to get Kenny ready for bed. Philippa was reluctant, perhaps she thinks no one else can prepare Kenny the way it's meant to be done. Stubborn sometimes, like Kenny could be. No one could wash his bike properly – not that I wanted to – and only he could make rice pudding like his mother's. That ticked me off as I considered it one of my own specialities, not that I ever complained; after all, the last time he'd have tasted his mother's rice pudding would have been when he was eleven, so it wasn't really the taste he wanted to recapture was it? But, yes, he could be stubborn. Like the time he took me and Philippa – she was not yet four – on holiday to a caravan site at Herne Bay. Caravan? Not really. More a big tin can with wheels. It started raining on the Sunday. By the Wednesday I'd had enough – the deluge on the thin metal roof was nearly enough to drown out both mine and Philippa's constant moaning. You couldn't blame us. We wanted to go home, but Kenny was stubborn to the point of stupid. We stayed until the Saturday. We didn't speak to each other until the following Monday, when I looked at him over tea and said, 'Still?'

After tea he mooched about the garden and came in with a barely flowering Michaelmas daisy – it was really too early in the season for them – which he simply handed to me, recited his rhyme and made me a cup of tea.

For years after, whenever he was being ridiculously stubborn I'd creep up beside him and whisper into his ear, 'Stubborn as a daisy.' Sometimes he laughed, sometimes he recited his rhyme, sometimes he pretended he was just about to change his mind anyway and sometimes he just stayed simply, well, stubborn. Eventually I learnt which fights to pick, and so did he.

Anyway, Philippa was hesitant to take up Kaska's suggestion, but it was already gone four and the commode and bathroom needed a proper disinfecting clean following Kenny's earlier mishap, and she was behind on some ironing, and Kenny would soon be wanting tea, and she wanted to wash her hair. Getting Kenny ready for bed before Kaska would arrive was going to be a challenge.

She took up Kaska's offer.

It's six forty. Philippa is in her bedroom, getting dressed. I'm waiting downstairs, with Kenny. We are watching the news. I don't know how much Kenny's taking in. Not too much I hope, it's depressing stuff. Not that we haven't been here before – I lived to be seventy-six and there was always a war somewhere or the economy was knackered or the government was useless or the unions were on strike or England had been knocked out of the cup or the post was late or the price of a loaf had gone up or the chippy by the station was turning into a Chinese takeaway or the hospitals were failing. That last one used to make Kenny smile. He remembered – better than I, he was five years older – before the National Health Service, when his dad had to pay the doctor to visit, and the midwife was the woman at the top of the road who'd had six children of her own. He remembered more about the war too. His oldest brother, John, didn't come back, so never-ending news reports about any war were both meaningless – he'd seen and heard it all before – and painful – he truly knew how loss felt, not only what it looked like.

Six forty-one: Philippa lets Kaska in then goes back upstairs to finish her hair. Kaska makes Kenny smile with a joke and a salute, and fiddles with the remote to find a cute Labrador puppy video on YouTube, telling Kenny one of her other clients watches it all day.

'All day?' asks Kenny.

'They are cute,' says Kaska.

'Nothing's cute enough to last all day.'

Kaska laughs.

'Besides,' says Kenny, 'I've got to go up the shops, and settle the coal bill. I'll take Blofeld.'

I think he's remembering when we lived with my mum and dad, and coal was delivered. We used to buy it from the National Coal Board. They had an office in the arches near the station. It was delivered in sacks from the back of a flat-bed lorry and the dirt-covered coalman had to heave them round the back to empty them into the coal bunker. I loved the smell. And, to be fair, the coalman wasn't dirty, he was sooty, which made his few teeth look much whiter than they were. He was always smiling – in my mind, at least.

'We can go up the shops tomorrow,' suggests Kaska.

'Why? Are you staying all night?' Kenny asks, then adds, 'I don't think my Beverley will like that.' He laughs mischievously. 'But I won't tell her.'

It's a good job I know he's joking.

Philippa comes down.

I hope Lewis is taking her somewhere nice. She's wearing dark blue trousers – a bit formal – and a pink, cotton blouse with a grey pinstripe. She carries a light woollen cardigan. Her hair is in a ponytail again. It still doesn't suit her. She looks anxious and walks a little uncertainly in heels she's not used to. I try to picture how tall Lewis is.

I know Ciaran might have liked how she's dressed and her hair, but he's not here, is he?

'You look lovely,' says Kaska. 'He must be taking you somewhere expensive.'

'Not really. Just for a drink.'

'Then it must be a nice pub. Not the ones I go to.'

'Am I over-dressed?' There is a hint of concern in her voice.

'No, not at all. Philippa looks lovely, doesn't she, Kenny?'

Kenny agrees, adding, 'But be back before dark and no boys.'

No one knows if he's joking but we all laugh.

Kaska starts, 'But …' then stops, then continues, '… such beautiful hair. Is a ponytail the best way?'

Thank you Kaska! It's what I've been saying all these years.

Philippa checks her watch, goes to the mirror in the hall, comes back into the lounge and asks Kenny if he likes her hair – of course he does. She goes upstairs and comes back down with her hair loose. Kaska tells her again how lovely she looks just as Lewis knocks on the door. Philippa grabs her cardigan, pecks Kenny on the cheek, tells him not to, 'Wait up,' and laughs. Kaska goes with her to the front door. I wonder what Lewis thinks of being greeted by two grinning women – one nervously, one mischievously. Make that three women. I, too, smile. Lewis leads her to his car, Kaska calls after them to have a nice evening.

I suppose I could go with Philippa but I won't. No daughter wants their mother on a date with them – is it a date? In my day we first walked out, and then went courting, but Hollywood and all that American music soon meant we were dating. Anyway, she doesn't need me there. In the early days of being dead, I'd go out with Kenny – shopping, hospital visits, walks round the block – but as he became gradually housebound and Philippa moved in, I've been out less and less, and now, well, now everything is a bit 'big' out there. Besides, I can't leave Kenny alone with a stranger, can I? And Kaska still is. A nice stranger, it seems, but still, a

103

stranger. Best I stay here.

Kaska and I sit with Kenny. She asks if he remembers the first time he went out with his wife. He looks confused so she brings in the photo album. He brushes my picture with a gentle finger and whispers, 'Beverley,' and I don't mind if he can't remember that first proper date.

The three of us have a quiet evening and Kaska does a great job of getting Kenny to bed. The routine isn't the same as with Philippa but she talks to Kenny all the time and he is quickly settled down.

Philippa is home by eleven. I'm waiting. Standing in Kenny's bedroom bay window, I can see Lewis walk her up the path and can hear them, despite Kenny snoring. They are close but not touching. The porch light is on. Philippa looks relaxed – I wonder if she had a lot to drink. She's not used to it. Lewis is wearing loafers, chinos and a plain white shirt with the cuffs turned up a couple of times. They look like office colleagues who went for a quick drink after work, stayed later than intended, are not sure why, but are glad they did.

'Thank you for the drink. It made a nice change.' Philippa turns as she takes the step to the door. She's now much taller than him.

'My pleasure, and thank you for the drink too.' Lewis sounds genuine. There is a pause and I hope neither of them is going to try and shake the other's hand. 'Next week?'

'Why not? It's good for me to get out.'

Lewis looks a little perplexed. I doubt that's the reason he hoped to hear. 'Perhaps a cocktail bar?'

'That would be nice, if I can get a sitter.' Philippa sees a hint of disappointment on Lewis's face. She adds, 'I'm sure Kaska will be available.'

Lewis takes this as a positive sign. 'Good, and let me know if you need anything from the shops over the weekend.' He stretches upwards, offering his face. Philippa bends over a little and they touch cheeks. Are they lip to cheek or cheek to cheek? I can't see from this angle but it's certainly not lip to lip. He pulls back just as Philippa turns her head for the other cheek – a double-cheek kisser? I never knew. Lewis, caught out a little but keen to match her, goes back forward and their faces collide just a little heavier than is comfortable. They both pull away and laugh. It's not a bad way to end an evening.

'How did it go?' Kaska gets to the question we've both been dying to ask as soon as she has finished the 'medical report' on Kenny's evening. We can hear him, still snoring contentedly. They are in the kitchen, waiting for the kettle to boil.

I can't tell if Philippa wants to talk about it or not. She was never one for giving away too much info about boys. Before she met Ciaran she had a few dates, and occasionally went out more than once with the same lad. But as far as I know she didn't go on the pill until after meeting Ciaran. She didn't tell me that, but I caught sight of the pack in her handbag. Not that I was searching through it, or even touched it, but what mum wouldn't cast a glance at her daughter's open bag, left on the kitchen table? I didn't ask her about it, or tell Kenny, but I was glad to see the pack. By then she was getting on for twenty and it was different times from our day.

'It was a nice evening. Had a drink, chatted easily enough. Did you know his new job is managing a regional area of window salesmen?'

'Er, no.'

'It's a lot more exciting than you might think.'

'Is it?'

'Not really,' Philippa laughs, 'but he does seem a nice guy, and we all have to earn a buck.'

Kaska looks confused.

That was one of Kenny's sayings: 'Gotta earn a buck.'

105

'More importantly,' Kaska asks, 'did he take your arm on the way into the pub? Did he find a reason to sit close? Did he press his leg against yours? Did you kiss? Apart from when saying goodnight I mean. Was he a gentleman?'

These are the right questions, thank you Kaska. But isn't she forward?

'Were you watching?' Philippa asks, half-seriously.

'Of course not. But your face is a little pink, so …'

'Well, we had a nice evening. He's a listener, not just a talker, has good manners, seems kind, has travelled a bit, and I do like his after-shave. It's like the stuff Ciaran saved for best that I bought him every Christmas. Paco Rabanne.'

Kaska nods and is about to ask another question when Philippa interrupts, 'I don't suppose it was much like your first date with Sophie. Where was that?'

More classic deflection.

Kaska smiles, I think in acknowledgement of the straight bat being played. 'She gave me her phone number at my brother's wedding and I waited a week before ringing.'

'Where did you go?'

'This was back in two thousand and two and our small town wasn't used to people like me and Sophie.'

'People like …? Oh.'

'So we met at one of the barns on the other side of the farm, where no one would go. It was a summer night. I took a bottle of wine, a blanket and a cassette player. Sophie brought beer and a cake. We drank, ate, danced to Madonna, and I sneaked back home after midnight …' Kaska fiddled with a thin silver bracelet I'd not noticed before. 'We didn't kiss until the next time. Then I knew I'd have to leave home. But …' Her voice fades.

They finish tea with a little more chat but no further revelations, and on the way to the door Philippa takes cash from her purse. I can't see how much. Kaska thanks her and points out it's more than the eight pound an hour they'd agreed.

Philippa gently dismisses the protest with a small hand

gesture – classic Kenny.

'The evening must have gone well,' teases Kaska. 'Will you go out with him again?'

'See you Monday, usual time?' Philippa side-steps the question.

The Michaelmas Daisy

Chapter 10
Monday 8th to Friday 12th July
One Day I'll Fly Away

The patio doors are open perhaps a foot, and, although it's raining hard, the fresher air is welcome. Kenny's watching stair rods crash into the shrubs and trees. The lawn is hard and brown, the rain pools, not soaking in. He's sitting upright in his riser/recliner and Philippa has tucked a light blanket around him. His face is pink, so I think he's warm enough. I wonder what he sees? Although he stares, it's not without interest, and he doesn't look like someone close to dozing off. The rain hammers on the plastic corrugated patio roof. I hope the din reminds him of that time in the tin caravan down at Herne Bay – stubborn as a daisy. Although I moaned at the time, I also remember sitting around the fold down table, drinking watery hot chocolate from plastic mugs and teaching Philippa how to play snap. Kenny made sure Pippa won and, to celebrate, we huddled under a waterproof groundsheet and shuffled over to the holiday park's social club. Next to the bar was a small grocery with a freezer. Philippa eventually decided on a Zoom lolly and I remember the lady at the till being so charmed by Philippa's polite request – I really did teach her to speak well – she said she could have it for a thrupenny bit instead of the usual fourpence.

Today's rain is even harder than back then – maybe there is something in the climate change talk I've been hearing – and the broken gutter can't handle the deluge. Gallons of water gush over the patio's edge. A few years back, Kenny would be out there, fixing it, rain or no rain.

The hammering on the plastic is satisfying, hypnotic, cosseting even, and Philippa stands at the patio door, duster in one hand, polish in the other, gazing out, much like Kenny. She's half-way through dusting the Lilliput Lane ceramics I collected and which, I know, are a cleaner's

109

nightmare. But there is something both comforting and dreamlike about them, especially the 2005 River Meadow Manor – a special collectors' edition, and a present from Kenny for our fiftieth anniversary. I miss handling them and finding new details to show Kenny. He was always interested, or at least, his pretence was convincing.

Philippa sighs. I wonder what she's thinking. I'm glad I don't know.

Kaska is bang on time, as we have come to expect. She's bedraggled from the rain, though she only had to run from car to porch. Her short blonde hair is plastered to her head. She leaves her wet sandals at the door and hangs her light mac on the hook in the hall. Philippa welcomes her with a towel and she takes a couple of minutes in the bathroom before joining Philippa in the lounge, greeting Kenny with, 'Holding the rails?' and a salute.

Kenny returns the salute and confirms, 'Holding the rails,' before asking Philippa, 'Who's this?'

Kaska laughs while Philippa explains.

'Remember,' adds Kaska, 'I'm the one that talks funny.' She laughs.

Kenny forces a smile but I think he's glad to see her.

Philippa puts on the kettle and brings two mugs of tea through to the lounge. She waits while Kaska sings 'Those Were The Days My Friend' to Kenny. He immediately picks up on the chorus. When they have finished, Kaska explains that another of her clients plays the song on repeat and she thought Kenny might know it. He does, sort of, well, the chorus at least.

We all sing it again, having to raise our voices against the volume of increasingly harder rain on the patio roof. Philippa tells Kaska that she's not going out today. Instead she'll be up in her room, painting, what with the terrible weather and all. Kaska says that's a good idea and asks what Philippa's painting.

'A portrait,' says Philippa.

'Of?'

Philippa hesitates, then, 'I'm not sure, yet.'

'Not sure? But a portrait?' Kaska is sceptical, so am I. 'Well we look forward to seeing it finished, don't we, Kenny?'

So do I.

'If it's any good,' offers Philippa.

Kaska indicates to the painting of Palma Cathedral. 'We don't doubt it. Do we Kenny?'

'No,' says Kenny though it's unlikely he has followed the conversation. Feeling Philippa and Kaska looking his way he adds, 'You're my daughter,' and holds a hand out to Philippa, smiling. She holds it tenderly for a minute and they sing the chorus to 'Those Were The Days My Friend' again.

Philippa goes up to her room. I stay with Kenny and Kaska. I have a rule about never entering Philippa's bedroom. It's been that way ever since she was a teenager and I walked in on her while she was … er, idolising? adoring? … a poster of David Essex. She was … adoring … him so intensely she didn't see me and I was back out the door sharpish. I was just pleased it was Essex and not Donny Osmond. I didn't mention it to Kenny, she was still his Pippa. It was hard enough telling him about her first period. I don't remember 'adoring' anyone famous when I was fifteen, but then we had the likes of Bing Crosby and Frank Sinatra. Come to think of it, I don't remember ever 'adoring' at all when I was a teenager, but I gather from what's on TV these days that not only is there a lot of it going on, it's ok to talk about it. In some instances it's actively encouraged – both the talking and the 'adoring'.

We have a peaceful forty-five minutes while Philippa is upstairs. Kaska finds Radio 2 on the TV. She shows Kenny her colouring book and he has a go. He does well, nearly staying within the lines, and is pleased when Kaska tells him so. They chat easily, or rather, Kaska keeps him engaged with easy questions. She makes sure to help him take small

111

sips from his Tommee Tippee mug and breaks a biscuit into small pieces. There are no toileting emergencies and Kenny only has to be reminded to swallow a couple of times. The rain eases and the sun is close to breaking through.

It's been a good afternoon.

'I need to cut the grass when it's dry,' says Kenny, concentrating intently on the garden.

'We'll get you out there soon,' says Kaska.

Kenny smiles broadly at this. He has been stuck in this house for a long time.

Philippa comes down as the hour is nearly finished. She's wearing one of Kenny's old work shirts. The sleeves are rolled up. It's spattered and streaked with paint.

'Very stylish,' says Kaska. 'Very, what's the word, bohee … something?'

'Bohemian? More plain scruffy. From the noughties school of British art,' says Philippa.

'Naughties?'

'Noughties,' repeats Philippa though that, of course, is no help whatsoever.

Kaska shrugs. 'Oh, and do you need me to sit with Kenny this Friday? Are you seeing Lewis again?'

'I'm not sure. I'd like to get to know him better, but …'

'What? Before agreeing to go out again? Shouldn't it be the other way around?' Kaska laughs. 'You need another night out, and I need the money. Remember, only eight pounds an hour.'

'Ok, why not. I'll need to get back to Lewis …'

'I think there's a good chance he will say yes.'

Later, once the upstairs vacuuming is finished, the kettle descaled, more ready meals ordered, an email sent to the GP to ask if Kenny's last blood test results showed anything, and that button missing from Kenny's pyjamas found and sewed back on, we settle in the lounge. The rain has stopped and we have maybe an hour before needing to think about tea. Time to relax.

Philippa is sitting on a stool by Kenny's riser/recliner. She has Kenny's right hand in hers and carefully clips his fingernails. Kenny doesn't mind. His attention is on the TV – a troupe of kittens tumble over each other. The mother is trying to sleep.

'So, Dad,' says Philippa, 'Guess what. I'm going out with Lewis again.'

She sounds genuinely pleased, and so she should.

'That's good,' says Kenny, 'I might come with you.' He's not being funny.

'Or you could stay here and Kaska will keep you company. You won't be alone.'

Kenny looks up from the TV. 'Who's Kaska?'

Philippa explains.

Kenny looks serious. 'I don't need anyone. I'm all right on my own. I am all the time since Beverley's not here. When's she coming back?'

'You're never on your own, Dad.'

'Yes I am.'

'I know you think …' Philippa stops herself. There is nothing to be gained. Philippa changes to his other side and takes the other hand. On the index finger she clips too closely and catches the merest sliver of skin. It's enough for Kenny to snatch his hand away and exclaim that it hurts. Philippa apologises. Kenny's reluctant to give her his hand again, but is persuaded, eventually. It's not the fear of being cut. It's just that he doesn't believe he needs anyone to trim his nails, he is perfectly capable of doing it himself.

Philippa finishes and decides not to try using a file to smooth them off. She passes Kenny his Tommee Tippee mug but keeps hold of it so he doesn't try to sip too much. He tries to pull it from her. He doesn't need her help. Philippa lets him have it then says,

'Right, time to cut those toenails now.'

She's not wrong, I saw them this morning when she

was dressing him; proper claws they are.

'I'll do them later,' says Kenny.

Of course he can't.

'Best I do them now, Dad. While I have the clippers. Besides, leave it any longer and we'll have to start darning your socks where the nails have torn through.'

I used to hate darning socks. I wasn't very good at it and there was always a bunching of stitches which I'm sure must have been uncomfortable when he put shoes on. Not that he ever complained, though I did once find him down his shed, unpicking some of my darning to re-do it. He tried to hide it when he heard me come in and I didn't say anything.

'I wouldn't even let Beverley cut my toe nails,' he says curtly.

As if I'd have wanted to; as if I now wouldn't love to.

Philippa starts to remove one of his socks and I can see he tries desperately to move his foot out of the way, but the foot barely twitches. We know he's not had a stroke or been paralysed in an accident or anything. Why is it much of his body just won't work? The strain on his face is pitiful. Philippa leaves his foot alone. Her mouth is tight, there is much she wants to say. There is nothing that will make a difference, so she takes a deep breath, hugs him as best she can, kisses his cheek, and makes all the difference in the world.

I look away. So much for watching over them. I watch over the painting of Palma Cathedral instead. It's a glorious building but my God doesn't need to be worshipped – I said that before, didn't I? He doesn't need Kenny and Philippa to pray to him. They need him more than he needs them. He owes them more than they owe him. Perhaps sending Philippa is his devotion to Kenny? But what about Philippa? Who is devoted to her, save me?

It has been a busy week, a week of anticipation, and I'm glad it's Friday. I'm sure Philippa's looking forward to this evening.

Kaska is settling in the lounge with Kenny while Philippa finishes dressing. She comes down to find Kaska and Kenny both have colouring books. Kaska's has intricate patterns and Kenny's is a child's but he doesn't mind. They are both concentrating. Mary Hopkin is singing 'Those Were The Days My Friend' on YouTube on the TV and Kenny joins in with the chorus. When it finishes, Kaska plays it again.

It's a warm summer evening and the patio doors are open. Movement in the garden catches my eye. That black cat is skulking down the bottom of the garden.

Philippa stands in the doorway, watching – I allow myself – all three of us, perhaps in a motherly fashion.

There is a loud knock on the door. Kaska looks up and nods approvingly at Philippa – her hair is not in a ponytail and she wears jeans and a polo shirt. The jeans sit on her hips and I wonder if the style is a bit 'young', but her legs are long enough for it to work, and she ordered a pair of special 'hold it all in' knickers which make a difference, to confidence if nothing else, I'm sure. She looks radiant and smells fresh and expensive – perhaps at last that bottle of Chanel No. 5 we bought her for Christmas has been used. Can expensive perfume last eight years? That was my last Christmas, and though I was confined to bed and drugged almost to comatose, I do remember Kenny, Philippa and Ciaran sitting on my bed as we exchanged gifts. We gave Philippa perfume, suggested by Ciaran. Kenny was amazed by the price, but happy to pay it. Kenny bought me a puppy, sort of. He adopted one at a local rescue centre in my name and we all laughed when I said I didn't think Beverley was a good name for a puppy. He was a cheeky looking mongrel. We decided on Banjo. Kenny was adamant he'd take me to meet Banjo in the spring. He believed it at the time. I'm not sure about Philippa, but I did catch Ciaran's eye and he knew I'd never meet Banjo. I wonder if Kenny's still paying the monthly sub? I hope someone adopted Banjo and he's romping around a big back garden, chasing balls thrown by kids.

That Christmas, I asked Philippa to buy Kenny an Airfix model of a Morris Traveller from me, our first car – something to keep him occupied when I was no longer around. I don't think he ever got round to making it. Last I saw, it was in a dresser cupboard with those old board games. Totopoly anyone?

Anyway, tonight Philippa looks and smells lovely. I hope Lewis knows how lucky he is.

Philippa pecks Kenny on the cheek and leaves us to a lazy evening. All goes well until eightish, when Kaska tries to convince Kenny it's time for bed. He's against the idea. Kaska backs off, after all he's a grown adult and knows when he's tired. But an hour later, when Kaska tries again, he's still resistant. Of course he doesn't realise it will take a good half hour to run through the routine – hoist, wheelchair, bedroom, hoist, part undress, commode, finish undress, bathrobe on, bathroom, toileting, strip wash, back to bedroom, hoist, dress for bed, bed, teeth out – but Kaska doesn't force the issue. It's another forty minutes before he can be gently coaxed. He's only just in bed when I hear movement at the front door. I slip behind the bay window curtain to watch.

Lewis is standing on the porch step so he's now a couple of inches taller than Philippa. They are hugging, but loosely. I can't hear what they are murmuring. Lewis pulls away just enough that he can angle his face to kiss her on the lips. She doesn't resist. The porch is in shadow and though I can't be sure, the kiss is not lingering. I doubt there were tongues involved. Should there be by now? On a second date? I don't know, these are different times to mine. We waited all the way until the third. I have a feeling Philippa might have expected some kissing, hence the fancy new electric toothbrush delivered by Amazon earlier in the week.

Philippa pulls away and there is muted talk. I get the impression they are pleasantries, though it's not awkward.

Philippa says something, Lewis nods agreement, and they co-ordinate a two-cheek kiss. He says he had a lovely time. Philippa agrees and waits until he has reached the gate before opening the door.

I slip from behind the curtains back into Kenny's room. He's on his back – he always sleeps that way, not having the strength to turn himself. There is just enough light from the hallway that I can see he's still awake, staring at the ceiling, occasionally muttering. I stand over him and look into his face. He smiles faintly, or do I imagine that?

Philippa pops her head into the room. From there she can't see Kenny's face and will likely think he's asleep. She takes half a minute to watch him. When she was a baby, and also into childhood, Kenny and I often stood at her bedroom door, watching and listening to her breathe; a calm, deep sleep of which I was envious. No, not envious. That might imply I'd not want that for her. Of course I did. I prayed that she might always sleep deep and easy. But I can't deny I didn't also pray for such sleep for myself. I used to sleep well, before Sasha and Philippa, but afterwards, never easy again.

Years later, Philippa told me, a little embarrassed, that she often lay awake at night, watching Ciaran and listening to him stir – so maybe my prayers for her weren't answered, though she said it was because she loved him.

I am suddenly sad on realising how much I miss watching her sleep when she was young. Maybe I should go into her bedroom one night, to watch again, but what if she's not sleeping? What if she's staring at the ceiling? Like Kenny.

'Beverley? That you?' Kenny has sensed her presence. I'm devastated it's not mine.

'No, Dad. It's Philippa,' she whispers.

'Come to bed, Beverley. It's late,' Kenny says to what

must be, to him, a silhouette. 'I'm cold.'

'Ok, Kenny, just doing my teeth,' she says, then pulls the covers higher to his neck and backs from the room.

'Put them in the glass next to mine,' says Kenny, laughing quietly.

'Love you,' says Philippa.

'You too,' Kenny replies.

Kaska is watching a film but heard her come in and smiles a welcome as she asks how the evening went.

'Lovely,' says Philippa.

We – me, Philippa and Kaska – are sitting in the lounge. They're drinking tea. It's close to eleven. Kaska is paid only to half-ten but doesn't seem to mind. Although it's getting late, the patio door is still open a little. The TV is off but I think a neighbour's having a party as dance music drifts in, never loud and always distant on some breeze.

'Saturday Night Fever,' says Philippa.

Kaska looks at her.

'Bee Gees? John Travolta? I danced to this when I was a teenager. Before your time.'

'Ah, yes.' Kaska tries the Travolta pose with raised hand and pointed finger; tricky when sitting down with a mug in the other hand.

Philippa laughs and asks, 'Did Dad go to bed ok?'

'Oh yes. He was fine,' she fibs.

'He was still awake when I looked. I watched him for a while. He once told me that he and Mum would stand at my bedroom door just to watch me sleep. It probably sounds stupid but, sometimes, when I'm in bed, but not quite asleep, sometimes, now and again, it feels like Mum is just outside.' Philippa smiles with faint embarrassment and sips her tea. 'When I popped in on Dad earlier he thought I was Mum.'

Philippa's chatty this evening. I wonder if she's had more to drink than usual, not that she has a 'usual' amount.

'He misses her. How long were they married?' Kaska asks.

I call out the answer. Philippa works it out and agrees, 'Fifty-six years.'

They sit in silence, perhaps considering what fifty-six years being married might feel like. It's easier to explain what it doesn't feel like, as I doubt there's a single emotion we didn't experience at some time or another. Kenny once said that we should know it all, good and bad, before we pass 'cos we're not coming back. He's right, and I don't regret anything, except having to grieve for Sasha. One regret. Not so bad after fifty-six years I suppose, except that one regret is enough for a lifetime, and beyond, so it turns out.

'Fifty-six years,' repeats Kaska, 'longer than I've been alive.'

'And nearly as long as I have been,' says Philippa.

'How old are you? Can I ask?'

'Fifty-nine.'

'You don't look past forty-five, honest,' says Kaska.

'I wish.'

'Which is why Lewis asked you out, I'm sure. And it was a lovely evening?' Kaska is fishing for information. I do like Kaska.

Philippa nods. 'We went to the new cocktail bar in the high street. I had a couple of margaritas. So expensive. We were the oldest there by at least twenty years, so we sat in the corner.'

'And how was Lewis?'

'He's ok. Though a couple of times he mentioned I'm quite tall. Perhaps it worries him.'

'No, surely not. I was a lot shorter than Sophie,' says Kaska, 'but it didn't matter, though I suppose it's different for girls. Once, in Paris, maybe two thousand and five, we were walking the Champs-Elysees, holding hands, and an ice cream salesman thought I was her younger sister. So I gave Sophie a kiss. A proper kiss. He wouldn't sell us the ice cream after that.' Kaska laughs and shrugs.

'I suppose you've had that a lot, over the years?'

'It was worse when we were so happy it was obvious.'

Philippa thinks about that for a few seconds. 'Jealousy?'

'I suppose.'

Philippa looks to have another question on her mind.

Kaska asks hers first, smiling broadly, 'So, Lewis? Do you fancy him?'

'Fancy? Isn't that for teenagers?'

'Do you think? Does he fancy you?'

'I don't think so, not in a … you know … really *fancy* way.'

I'm not sure I know what Philippa means but Kaska seems to, and asks, 'Would you like him to?'

'I don't know, but I guess it would be nice if someone did, wouldn't it?'

I wonder how big those margaritas were.

'Would it?' Kaska prompts.

'I suppose. It's been a long time and … I guess a … cuddle with someone, anyone would be something. It's been such a long time.' Philippa hesitates, then continues, as if compelled. Those margaritas must have been double measures. 'But beyond a cuddle? I don't know. I've forgotten how.' It nearly comes across as a joke.

'It hasn't changed. I'm sure it would all come back to you. If you fancy him,' Kaska teases. 'So do you?'

'I think I'm a little tall for him.' Philippa swerves the question.

'Well, in that case we need to find a man who's taller. Maybe fancy him instead.'

The party music has been turned up. They listen for a minute. The music is slow.

'Another from my era. Must be smooch time,' says Philippa, 'I danced to this at my wedding. 'One Day I'll Fly Away'. It was our second dance.'

I remember. They were a lovely couple dancing to a

lovely tune but it's no 'Unforgettable', is it? That's the one me and Kenny danced to. Nat King Cole; can't go wrong.

'Do you know it?' Philippa asks.

Kaska shakes her head.

'Probably before you were born. I bet you could almost be my daughter.'

Kaska hesitates and sips on her tea. Her smile fades. I think she's weighing up her sentence, 'No grandchildren for Kenny?'

An interesting way of phrasing the half-question. Philippa shakes her head and shrugs.

Kaska waits to see if there is any further explanation but when none is forthcoming adds, 'I have no children. I wanted to, but Sophie didn't. Of course it would be difficult, two women, I know, but I have friends who made arrangements. It only needs a man willing to ... you know, and they aren't hard to find. But children were not for Sophie. I understand, but she would have been a great mama. I have had other girlfriends since, but not like Sophie. I don't know how to make them last. It's tiring to not be settled. And I'm moving again, soon, I think.'

Kaska's voice fades and neither Philippa nor I know what to say. I haven't seen Kaska look sad like this before.

Philippa though? Yes.

The Michaelmas Daisy

Chapter 11
Monday 15th July
Cutting The Grass

I'm standing at the open patio door, watching Philippa cut the grass. The garden looks tidy at first sight but a practised eye knows better. The shrubs need trimming, there is dead-heading to be done, the bird bath is dry, and there are a couple of lumps of cat mess only half-buried in the raised flower bed – that black cat I expect – but I won't mention any of this to Philippa, after all, the garden looks quite lovely and she's doing a great job; I would tell her. There is a cover of white cloud, keeping the day warm rather than hot, and I think the birds must be resting as the only sounds are the TV – Kenny's sort of watching *Loose Women* – and the tumbling grind of the mower's blades as they rev up then slow then rev then slow as Philippa puts her weight into pushing then pulling. It's a satisfying, gravelly, mechanical noise, accompanied by bursts of cut grass thrown into the air, some of it even landing in the basket attached in front of the blades. Philippa uses the old Qualcast mower that we bought when we first moved in. It's hard work for her. It wasn't hard for Kenny back then, that's why he stubbornly refused to buy an electric one, even when it became hard work for him too. Stubborn as a daisy.

I love the smell of cut grass and remember the times spent in the park watching the small tractor pull the agricultural blades over the bright green lawns. I especially remember the height of summer, when the council sent entertainers to keep the kids, er, entertained. They were mostly magicians, and when the small maroon coloured van, with the proud council crest on the side, drove slowly into the park, the children would run alongside. When it stopped they would instinctively sit on the grass, forming a half-circle at the van's side. Us mums would gather in an outer half-circle of our own, like a wagon-train, protecting the squatting children as they waited, not always patiently. The driver and accomplice would step from the van, their faces switching from tired acceptance to an entertainer's bright smile, almost natural, in an instant. Yes it was a job for them, but I think they enjoyed it. I think it made a difference. The short skits and magic acts made us laugh and sing along, and the kids who were persuaded to help with the tricks were never belittled – well, maybe just a little to get a laugh, but then they were given a lollipop. When they asked for volunteers, Philippa's arms was first to shoot in the air and she was called up a couple of times, thrilled and bemused when a coin appeared from behind her ear or a rope she had just cut in two was magically whole.

They were happy summers. The only minor regret was that Kenny was at work and couldn't join us.

I look over my shoulder and nearly ask him if he likes the smell of the grass. I do – I said that already didn't I? – but also, I don't. Kenny had cut the grass that Saturday in July, ten years ago, just before I'd told my bad news. He cut it again after I'd spoken, leaving it to Philippa and Ciaran to ask the questions and offer sympathy. Not that Kenny didn't care, but the shock was deep and immediate, and forcing that old Qualcast across the lawn in regimented strips was a comfort of sorts; a control, of sorts.

I'd actually learnt my bad news the day before, but held back telling it until the Saturday, knowing Philippa and Ciaran would be popping over. I couldn't face telling it twice. It was difficult to pretend to Kenny there was nothing wrong when I'd come out of the consultant's office – I hadn't wanted Kenny in there with me – and of course Kenny knew me well enough to understand there was a problem. He also knew enough to appreciate that I would give the news in my own way, and at a time of my choosing, but that Friday night was perhaps the worst of my life, especially in bed. We both pretended to sleep.

So, that July Saturday in 2009, I remember vividly, I tried to tell Philippa and Kenny about my cancer with a lack of melodrama. I nearly got away with it until Philippa asked where it was and how far advanced. I couldn't lie: pancreas and very.

She glanced at Ciaran. He knew what 'pancreas and very' meant, and though I suppose he and Philippa were already having 'marital' problems, there was still that bond, meaning he could convey to her the seriousness with the merest of expressions. So, a second after Ciaran understood, so did she. I'm not sure Kenny did at first, but Philippa was not able to hide her horror quickly enough, and, seconds later, Kenny knew too.

'Sorry, Mum?' she had asked in order that I'd repeat the news. She always was one for double-checking.

'I need to finish that grass,' Kenny had said, leaving me, Philippa and Ciaran in the kitchen.

I have mixed feelings about the smell of newly cut grass.

If the night before I told them was the worst of mine and Kenny's lives, the night afterwards was one of the best. Kenny held me until morning and we lay awake through the night, saying little but sharing everything. I think Kenny already knew he could do nothing to stop the inevitable, but he also knew how to be strong enough to make sure I understood he loved me, would not flinch from looking me in the eye, would not lie to me, would never leave me and could help us be ourselves to each other in a way we hadn't needed to before.

I died on the fifteenth of July, 2011, a little over two years after telling Philippa and Kenny the news, and eight years to the day that I now stand here watching Philippa mow the lawn while Kenny watches *Loose Women*. It was an awful two years; it was a liberating two years; I was mostly scared and occasionally proud that I was able to pretend to be so brave; it was two years I wished I hadn't had to live through; it was two years I'm glad I did, if only it could have been in a decade still to come. The worst of it, no surprise, was towards the end, as my body shut down but my mind was still alive and not totally dulled by drugs. Those were the days of pain and realisation; a realisation I can't explain; I don't want to try – it's a dark, cruel, horrific, terrifying realisation, and I won't go back there. But I have no memory of the final few days, as my body gave up one organ at a time. I'm pleased not to remember. I came through it. So did Kenny. We can be proud again, can't we?

Does Philippa remember today is the anniversary of my death? Why is she cutting a lawn that doesn't really need it? I wonder if she'll mention the anniversary to Kenny. I hope so, though I'd rather she didn't.

It's getting on lunchtime. Philippa has tidied away the Qualcast without wiping the blades, never mind, they are already blunt after all these years. Kenny would gently chide her if he knew. In the lounge she's dusting the Lilliput Lane ceramics even though there is still some ironing to be done and Kenny's bed hasn't been made. Kenny's dozing. The home phone rings.

As usual, frustratingly, I can only hear one side of the conversation. I piece together what I can. The caller is April and the only April I know is the brusque but kind Scottish lady who manages the local community centre. After some pleasantries, during which Philippa offers congratulations on a baby – I guess a grandchild, surely – and fibs about meaning to get Kenny down to the centre for one of the seniors' day clubs, I hear Philippa giving thanks for, 'Being thought of,' agreeing that, 'Yes, twenty-two an hour is more than fair,' and promising to, 'Think it over and get back to you in a day or two.'

I dearly want to know what that's about.

Philippa finishes dusting River Meadow Manor with new-found enthusiasm.

'Dad,' Philippa whispers and gently shakes Kenny awake.

'What?'

'Lunch. Cheese sandwich, no crusts, cup of tea.' Philippa indicates to the wheeled table within Kenny's reach. He doesn't look enthusiastic. Perhaps he's still tired.

Philippa flicks through a few channels and finds a programme about renovating a house. She asks if he wants to watch it. He shrugs his shoulders and they sit in silence for a few minutes before Philippa says, 'Guess what, Dad, I've been offered a job.'

Kenny looks at her. I sneak closer. What have I missed?

'The community centre wants me to teach the art class there, like I used to. How good is that?' Philippa is excited.

So it *was* April from the community centre on the phone earlier. This is exciting news. Philippa sounds genuinely pleased, and so she should. Never mind the extra money, it's nice to be thought of and asked; every bit as nice as it is to know you're not forgotten.

'Good,' says Kenny, 'We all need to work. I'm going back in tomorrow.' He's not being funny.

'It's one evening a week, running the art class again,' explains Philippa. 'Remember I used to, when I first came home?'

Kenny doesn't – as Philippa well knows – but nods anyway.

'I could ask Kaska to come and keep you company. You won't be alone. I'd have to pay her, but will still make enough to buy some more materials for my own painting and it'll get me out a bit more. Besides, I don't want to let them down and, anyway, it's nice to be asked. Really nice.'

That's just what I said. It's a joy to see Philippa looking so, well, joyous. She was – will be – a very good art teacher. Perhaps it means she'll finish that portrait upstairs.

Kenny looks up from the TV. 'Who's Kaska?'

Philippa laughs but doesn't explain. Instead she tells him, 'I just heard Lewis's car pull in. I'm popping next door. Won't be a minute.' She's half-way to the door – I'm not happy she's leaving Kenny on his own, even for a minute – when she returns and moves the table with his lunch on it out of reach before going out again.

Philippa's back in less than five minutes. I wait for her to tell Kenny why she needed to talk to Lewis, but she doesn't, and they finish lunch in silence.

She tidies up the kitchen, checks the post that has just arrived, tries to ring the gas board – or whoever they are now – to ask why they've increased the direct debit, but gives up after a fifteen minute wait because Kenny needs the toilet – hoist, gloves, commode, bathroom, clean etcetera, etcetera, etcetera – then rings the doc to see if they'll come round to look at the rash on Kenny's back which is getting worse, but the doc is too busy and the receptionist says ring back tomorrow. So Philippa finishes some ironing, makes Kenny's bed, orders some new vests for him from Amazon and goes through his top drawer to throw out those that are threadbare. She makes him a fresh squash and takes it through to the lounge, helping him with the first delicate sip to make sure there's a strong swallow. Kenny nibbles on the biscuit – not chocolate these days – while Philippa tries to find some YouTube videos of a train ride. She does so then notices some dust on one of the higher shelves on the dresser. She brings a duster and polish in from the kitchen and moves the casket from the shelf. The casket. My casket. She takes a second to read the engraved plate, even though she has read it a thousand times. She puts the duster down and checks her watch, catches a breath. Does it occur to her that today is the anniversary of my death? It's exactly eight years to the day – well, in an hour or so.

I am a little disappointed she hasn't remembered, but not surprised. I am not bitter. Truly. She has such little time for herself, let alone me.

She glances over at Kenny. She suddenly looks tired,

drawn and heavy. Weary. She starts to say something but Kenny's denture drops out of his mouth and into his lap. He looks at it, surprised. Philippa wipes the duster over the shelf and casket then replaces it so she can go and help Kenny who is examining the denture.

She's in the kitchen, washing her hands when her phone rings. I hear her side and can guess what this one is about. She returns to the lounge to tell Kenny: the optician is coming a little earlier than planned, in only twenty minutes. Kenny nods. It makes no difference to him.

The optician seems nice enough. Philippa shows her through to the lounge and she sets up some equipment. Kenny's chair is raised so he's sitting upright. He's not relaxed.

'Mr Cooper?' the optician calls, to gain his attention.

Kenny, without his spectacles, looks at Philippa. She nods.

'Can you see the letters?' The optician is a few feet away, pointing to a sight chart hanging from a flimsy collapsible stand.

Kenny nods but doesn't speak. The optician asks him to read the first three rows. He shakes his head.

'Can you not see them, Dad?' Philippa asks.

'Of course I can.'

'Can you tell us what the letters are?' The optician is firm but kind.

'I don't need new glasses. I don't want them,' Kenny tells Philippa.

The optician pretends to smile and sits in the armchair near to him. 'How long have you had those, Mr Cooper?' She indicates to the spectacles held by Philippa. 'Can I call you Kenny?'

'No.'

The optician's smile doesn't falter. 'Not to worry, but how long have you had them? Perhaps you need a new pair.

I can help.'

'I don't need help.'

'Three or four years.' Philippa answers the question. 'Time for new ones, Dad.'

'I don't need them.'

Philippa and the optician exchange looks.

The optician picks up the photo album from the side table and places it in Kenny's lap.

'I bet there are some lovely photos in here, Mr Cooper. Wouldn't you like to see them better?'

'I can see them fine.'

'Can you?' The optician opens the album, flicks through and finds a black and white group photo. It's quite small. Chosen, no doubt, for the optician's purpose. 'Who's in this one?'

Kenny looks at it. Of course it's not a fair question. He's not wearing his spectacles. I'm torn between wanting to defend him but also recognising he does need his eyes testing.

The optician turns the page and asks again, 'Who're they?'

Kenny doesn't look at the picture.

It's a photo of his niece and nephew. Kenny's with them in his brother's garden. This is the middle brother, Freddy. The picture is probably twenty-five years old. It's at least that long since Philippa last saw the cousins, at their granddad's cremation. They are a little older than her, in their sixties now. We haven't heard from Freddy for years, since that … disagreement.

'Are they your grandchildren?' The optician is determined to engage.

Kenny gives a cursory glance.

'He doesn't have grandchildren,' says Philippa.

'Yes I do,' says Kenny, finally checking the photo.

'No you don't, Dad,' says Philippa.

'Of course I do.' He's angry.

'But …' Philippa hesitates.

'Anyway, how would you know?' There is cruelty in his words.

Philippa is shocked into silence, so am I. She apologises to the optician and leaves the room.

The optician has gone. The sight test was unsuccessful but they agreed to try again in a week or two – 'cos a couple of weeks is going to make a difference, right. Perhaps I am becoming bitter; about so many things.

Kenny's still in the lounge. Philippa is in the kitchen, searching the freezer for the Bolognese she made a few weeks ago. There is no enthusiasm in the task. I don't blame her, it's been another exhausting day. The phone rings and she answers reluctantly. It's Kaska, and I gather she's ringing to confirm tomorrow's visit. Philippa is a little curt; bordering on rude even. The call is brief as she has to get back to the microwave.

Fifteen minutes later, Kenny's eating dinner in the lounge, Philippa's watching, she's not hungry. The knock at the front door is a nuisance.

It's Kaska. She has just finished another job, round the corner, and is on her way home, so thought she'd pop in for a cup of tea. I'm sure Philippa's glad to see her but struggles to raise a smile.

Kaska goes straight through to the lounge. 'Good afternoon, Kenny.' She gives him a salute. He looks up from his barely touched Bolognese but doesn't respond. 'Holding the rails?' she asks.

'Just about.' There is no humour in his reply.

'Tiddlywink Old Man …' Philippa tries. It's usually a safe bet to tease a smile from him.

Not today. Kenny neither responds nor smiles. Philippa asks him if he'd like a cup of tea. He shakes his head. Philippa goes out to the kitchen. Kaska follows. She and Philippa stand at the sink, waiting for the kettle to boil.

'Garden looks nice.' Kaska says, eventually. 'Maybe we

can get Kenny out there one day.'

'It's not how it should be, but ...'

'It's still nice. I haven't got a garden. A plant pot on a balcony helped, until my ... flatmate ... took it to grow weed.'

I think Kaska's comment is worthy of a question but Philippa just nods.

'And how has Kenny been today?' asks Kaska, and the three of us know she's really asking how Philippa is.

'It's been a ... tricky day,' says Philippa, though she's saved from having to explain by the boiling kettle. Tea is made in the cups – what's wrong with my teapot? They take their drinks to sit at the kitchen table. Kaska takes two mini Milky Ways from her bag, offers one to Philippa who shakes her head.

'It must have been a very tricky day,' says Kaska, 'if the answer isn't chocolate.'

Philippa manages a thin smile. 'How was your day?'

'Only three clients. Not too busy. Not really busy enough. I need more work. That's not true. I really need more money, ha. But Mrs Tanner gave me this.' From her bag she brings out a tiny, knitted jumper – white with a rabbit on the front. 'Cute, eh?'

'Very. Bit small though.'

'Ha, that's what I said. But it's for my nephew. My brother's wife had another baby, just a couple of days ago. Here.' Kaska finds some photos on her phone and passes it to Philippa.

Philippa scrolls slowly through photos of a swaddled newborn with scrunched up face and quiff of dark hair. It's a cute baby, if not particularly pretty or handsome – if Kaska hadn't said, I wouldn't have known if it's a girl or a boy. Philippa looks at, but doesn't dwell on, each picture and offers suitably flattering comments. They carry less enthusiasm than they might. She finishes with, 'I expect your mum's very proud.'

'Oh yes. And since she couldn't rely on me to produce

a grandchild, my brother is the hero.' There's no humour in Kaska's tone.

'I'm sorry, I didn't mean to … you know.' Philippa looks into her mug. Her eyes are moist. She apologises, 'I'm sorry, I'm tired. It's been a tough day and when Dad said he's a grandad, it … it wasn't easy to hear, when he was so close. He would have been great, as a granddad.'

'He would. You and … whatshisname … wanted children?' Kaska's voice is almost a whisper, as if inviting Philippa to pretend she hasn't heard if she doesn't want to answer. I, of course, desperately want her to answer, but only if she wants to, of course.

Philippa doesn't respond. They drink in silence until Kaska prompts, 'A tricky day?'

Philippa nods and her eyes glisten a little more.

'You need a night out.' Kaska tries to sound positive. 'Any plans with Lewis?'

'Not really. We … he … agreed that maybe we should just be friends.'

'Friends?'

'As in, the occasional drink and catch up but that's it. I spoke to him today.'

'Oh. Did something happen?'

'I don't know.'

'And just friends isn't ok?'

'It's ok, and I'm not even sure I want something more. But I thought he did, and we might try and who knows. Turns out I was wrong. And I don't even mind that much, except, you know, it might have worked out and …'

'And as my mother says, "it's nice to be asked".'

Philippa forces a laugh. 'Mine used to say the same.'

I still do. And Lewis is an idiot. He should be so lucky as to be a friend, never mind anything more. Idiot.

'It has been a tricky day. A bad day.' Kaska leans forward and rubs Philippa's forearm. She doesn't flinch.

'And I forgot, Mum died eight years ago, to the day.' Philippa looks over to my photo. 'I forgot.' A tear wells onto

133

her cheek. She looks pale and small.

I shout at her, 'I don't care. I really don't care!'

'Oh. I didn't know. I'm sorry. Truly a bad day.' Kaska agrees but goes to the kitchen counter and brings back the picture of me at the beach. 'She would understand.'

'I know. But it doesn't help …' Philippa takes the picture, '… she laughed so much, and always with you, never at. That helped. She gave Dad and me her heart. She was Dad's heart, and I don't even know what that means. I feel awful I don't miss her all the time, but that's just too hard. It's easy and a comfort to remember how she was and what she did and how she made me feel and how she made things right, but it's different, and just too hard, to miss her, to know she'll never be or do those things again. It's too much …'

I feel my knees weaken; please, please, don't miss me; remember, smile, but don't miss.

'… so much, always …' mutters Philippa.

Philippa's words hang and I can see Kaska is thinking of what to say that might make a difference. Instead, we hear Kenny calling out, for me. We go to check on Kenny. Philippa kneels at his chair. Kenny looks up from his now cold, barely touched, Bolognese, takes a second to study Philippa and asks,

'Who are you?'

There is silence. The longest and deepest of my life and death.

Philippa stands to full height, laughs, walks to the patio doors, stares out to the garden for a few seconds, laughs again, whispers something about tea and leaves the room. But she doesn't go to the kitchen. Instead she goes to the rarely used front parlour, closing the door behind her. Her racking sobs are loud enough to be heard.

Kenny, Kaska and I wait in the lounge. Kaska is speechless, Kenny's oblivious, I am ripped apart.

I don't want to be – can't take – being dead like this anymore, as if the choice were mine.

Kaska opens the door to the front parlour cautiously. We both go in. It's cold in here, it doesn't get the sun like the lounge, and smells musty. Philippa is sitting on the sofa, hunched forward, hugging herself, sobbing. Her eyes try to blink away tears, her face is red and blotchy.

Kaska sits next to her, 'A bad day.'

Philippa says nothing but leans a little into Kaska who stretches an arm around her. It's not comfortable as she's so much smaller, but she pulls Philippa in. Philippa's cheek rests against Kaska's shoulder. Kaska puts her other arm around her and hugs her tightly, never mind how awkwardly.

It's an unnatural, unbalanced cuddle but it doesn't matter.

Philippa's sobs are a little easier. 'A bad day,' she echoes and leans a little heavier into tiny Kaska. I wonder, when was the last time Philippa was so close to someone, anyone? My daughter is lonely and sad and I feel so absolutely bloody useless. I wish there was another kind of dead, where I didn't have to feel this. But more, I pray my daughter won't have to. Where is my God? Where is Philippa's God?

Kaska starts to speak, but I think she realises there's nothing to be said that will help, and stops. Instead, she gently wipes a tear from Philippa's cheek.

They stay that way for a couple of minutes, I am an intruder. I check on Kenny. He has fallen asleep but I sit with him and ask, 'Oh, Kenny, what have you done?' and feel worse for blaming him.

I return to the front parlour. Philippa is no longer leaning into Kaska and has stopped crying. Her face is pink and the little mascara she was wearing has run. Kaska tries to wipe it away with a finger but makes it worse.

'... Lewis is a fool,' says Kaska, 'and Kenny does know you, even if he wasn't sure who you are, for a moment.'

'Thank you, but ...' says Philippa.

'And it was not all bad today. You got a job.'

Philippa has told Kaska about the call from April at the community centre.

'How can I go out for an evening if Dad can't even remember who I am coming back from the kitchen? I'll have to say no.' Philippa's tears return. Kaska hugs her again. It's another minute before Philippa stops. Kaska tries to make her laugh,

'I've never cuddled another woman that long without it leading to sex before. It doesn't feel weird at all,' she says.

'Not at all,' agrees Philippa. 'I wonder what Mum would say.'

I don't know what to say. If I was there this wouldn't need to happen. I'm not there.

'I wonder what my partner ... ex-partner would say,' says Kaska.

'Ex?'

'Officially as of today. So yes, it's a bad day.'

Philippa pulls away from her. 'Oh, I'm sorry ...'

'It's ok. It's been coming. She asked me to move out a while ago and today she's gone away for a while and I'm not to be there when she gets back. So, definitely a bad day.' It's now Kaska's turn to cry. Philippa turns a little on the sofa to be as face on to Kaska as possible. Their knees touch. Philippa takes both of Kaska's hands in both of hers and holds them tight. They bow their heads until their foreheads rest on each other.

Chapter 12
Friday 19th July
Bye Bye Blackbird

Friday, Kaska is ten minutes early. She walks into the lounge singing 'Those Were The Days My Friend'. Kenny's happy to see her and joins the chorus. He's brightened up since Monday. He knows who Philippa is far more often than he doesn't, and, even then, is relaxed. Some instinct tells him he should trust her. I'm not sure this is a great comfort to Philippa.

The house is neat and tidy – Philippa was up early. She's not sleeping well.

Kaska chats with Kenny. When Philippa brings him in a fresh drink, Kaska asks her, 'Did you accept the art class job yet?'

'Not yet, though the lady in charge did ring again. But I don't think it's for me.'

'Really?'

Philippa shrugs. Kaska's silence is an invitation for Philippa to continue.

'I'm still worried about leaving Dad. An hour during the day is one thing but three or four hours in the evening? I don't know … Dad isn't himself these days. He's having more … accidents. And he sometimes forgets who I am after just a few minutes, never mind a whole evening.'

'He always knows you are of him and for him,' says Kaska.

It's a strange way of putting it, but makes sense.

'Then there's the money,' says Philippa after thinking about what Kaska just said. 'It's ok, but after paying for a sitter …'

'I'll do it for ten pound an hour plus free drawing lessons. I want to learn.'

That would leave Philippa with twelve quid an hour. Not much these days, from what I gather, but it's the getting

137

out that's as important. Philippa smiles, 'I thought we'd agreed on eight?'

'That is date nights only.' Kaska smiles mischievously. The smile fades as she adds, 'Besides, I'm saving. I need to move out, remember?' She fiddles with her phone and passes it to Philippa, asking, 'Do you use Facebook?'

Philippa shakes her head, 'Not much.'

Of course I know what Facebook is. A few years before I fell ill, Philippa convinced me to try it and I even had my own page. I put up a few photos but I've not posted anything for years, haha. I wonder if anyone's missed me.

'See, they like it, very much.'

I look over Philippa's shoulder. Kaska's Facebook page shows a painting of Palma cathedral – Philippa's painting. Below the picture are a lot of comments, all complimentary, all praising the painting. Kaska points to one in particular,

'Josslyn loved it, and she makes a living from painting portraits. She even studied at a … what's it called … academy?'

Philippa scrolls down the page. She's a little embarrassed by the comments.

'So,' says Kaska, 'you should take the job at the art class.'

Philippa returns from her respite break. She looks worried but brightens up when Kenny recognises her and tells Kaska, 'That's my daughter.'

Philippa doesn't ask him for a name.

Kaska gives her usual formal update on Kenny's 'status'. It went well and no toileting was needed. But we noticed Kenny's swallowing is a little worse. Kaska chilled his orange squash in the fridge as cold drinks are better for swallowing, apparently.

Philippa says maybe the doctor will come out.

Kaska says goodbye to, 'MO Kenny,' and salutes.

Kenny does likewise. Philippa walks to the door with her. In the background they can hear Kenny singing, 'Bye Bye Blackbird' and both smile, then Philippa says, 'By the way, I'm sorry, I didn't ask you about having to move out of your flat. Not that it's any of my business and tell me if so, but …'

Kaska's smile is gone. 'It's ok. Two years is long enough to learn someone isn't the right someone. Time to move on.' Kaska doesn't sound convinced but laughs to pretend she is. 'And I get on well with a neighbour who has a big car and I haven't much stuff to move. So, just need to find another flat, and I've still got a week.'

Philippa doesn't know what to say. At the front door they exchange silent looks – pity on Philippa's part, sadness on Kaska's – then Philippa tells Kaska, 'I'm going to take the art teaching job. I can always stop if it gets too much, right?'

'Of course.'

I agree. Though I'm reminded of the time Ciaran volunteered to help out at a charity and convinced Philippa to join in. I don't think Philippa needed much persuasion. The charity helped local teenagers in need of practical help or some advice – homeless or addicted or young mums or jobless or bullied; all sorts. The charity was a first port of call, like a CAB for youths, and they'd help them find the right sort of help from the right organisation or authority. It also gave them a place to go where they weren't judged. Listen to me – I sound like an advert for it. I didn't understand at first, but Ciaran and Philippa told me some of the sad stories they heard and, I must admit, I was soon proud of them for giving their time. It started with an evening a fortnight but soon became once a week, then an evening and half a day on the weekend. When they started cancelling our monthly Sunday lunches, I hinted to Philippa it might be getting out of hand, but she insisted not – this would be summer of '98 or '99. Come autumn, I could see Philippa wasn't enjoying it as much and looking tired but she always said she'd stop if it got too much. By then I think it already had, but she carried on until Christmas. When she did pack it in, she said it wasn't because it was tiring, but that she found the increasing number of young mums with sad, sad stories just too much. Ciaran hinted she was on anti-depressants but I asked her and she denied it. I told her nothing wrong with them – half of us young mums were on 'mother's little helpers' back in the sixties – but she was quick to remind me she wasn't a young mum.

Back in the lounge, Kenny smiles at Philippa and asks, 'Who was that?'

Philippa looks at the pile of ironing and finds the resolve to ignore it. She sits next to Kenny, takes his hand and sings 'Bye Bye Blackbird'.

Chapter 13
Monday 5th August
We'll Meet Again

Philippa starts teaching at the art centre in just a couple of days and I sense both the excitement and nerves. She's taught art before and was, I've no doubt, good at it. Sitting at the dining room table, she flicks through her old text books and a coffee table book of famous paintings. They are beautifully reproduced on expensive paper. It was a present to herself when she finished her apprenticeship. Kenny's in his recliner, folding and refolding a napkin from perfect triangle to perfect square and back. Classic FM is on the telly-radio, and the violins – I've no idea what they are playing – are calming, almost as calming as watching Kenny's origami.

Philippa has bought a reporter's pad and is making notes under the heading: Light. I look to the paintings of Palma cathedral and Brighton Pavilion. It's a topic she knows well, as far as I can tell.

Every twenty minutes or so, Philippa will go across to Kenny and put the Tommee Tippee mug to his lips, encouraging a small sip. Kenny's always happy to see her when he looks up from his napkin. I pretend I am there with them – which I am, but you know what I mean – sitting in my armchair, tray on my lap, finishing a puzzle. It's the puzzle that has been in our family for years. I don't remember if it came from my side or Kenny's. The picture is of an ocean liner. It has a dark blue hull and four mustard-coloured funnels, two of which belch white smoke. The sea is calm and dark green, save for the white foam frothing at the bow. The sky is orange and magenta. Perhaps it's sunset. Good use of light, I tell Philippa, like I know anything about art. I imagine the guests on board are just going down to the bar for their evening cocktails. They will be dressed immaculately and stylishly. The manners of the time force

141

trivial small-talk between the women and men, but it doesn't cause coldness; it builds the tension between them into something sensual.

I wish Kenny and I had taken a cruise – a ferry to Calais doesn't count, though we did have a good day and brought back a duty-free bottle of cream sherry, which might still be in the sideboard.

The puzzle's picture is of the *RMS Titanic* and, as I mentioned, it's been in the family for decades, coming out every other year or so for completion. It's lost three pieces, just where I think the bridge would have been – as if I'd know. I wonder if that's why it hit an iceberg, because the captain was missing, haha.

Kenny looks up, something in the garden has caught his notice. I don't see it. I try to catch his attention by asking, 'Ok, Kenny? Holding the rails?' Who knows, one day he may answer, though it strikes me that might be because he's just crossed over to my side, and what would I do if that happened? It's a wonderful, exciting, intoxicating thought which I quickly suppress. I have learnt that it doesn't do to be too optimistic when you're dead.

Kaska arrives, on the button. She is less 'smiley' than usual. Philippa, excited, tells her plans for the opening lesson, explaining that, 'Without shadow, there is no light.'

'That maybe in pictures,' says Kaska, seriously, 'but in life is it not the other way? We need the light to show us what's in the shadows.'

I'm not sure what she means, but think there's some truth there, somewhere. Philippa looks thoughtful.

Kenny calls from the lounge, 'Bev! That you?'

Philippa and Kaska join him. Kaska has a new song to find on YouTube – one of her clients loves Vera Lynn. Soon we are all singing 'We'll Meet Again'. The words are on the screen. It's a bit maudlin for me, but then I was only ten when the war finished. None of my close relatives died in it, and my dad was in a reserved occupation – engineering – so didn't leave home. When I was older, I wondered how he felt about that. Did he feel guilt, or some misguided shame that he hadn't fought directly? But I never asked him. It was not a question to ask, in case the answer was yes. No dad needs those feelings brought back, especially in front of his daughter.

'I'm not going out today,' Philippa tells Kaska.

'On such a day?' Kaska indicates to the garden. 'It's so nice. We must get Kenny out there while it's still summer. Don't you agree, MO Cooper?' Kaska takes Kenny's hand. He hasn't been listening but nods.

'It is, but I need to practice some brush work, which I can do upstairs,' says Philippa.

'Ah, on the picture of the someone that you don't know it will be yet.'

Philippa looks apologetic.

I wonder why the portrait is a secret? I'll pop in one day, perhaps next time she's out.

'Are you looking forward to your new job?' Kaska asks.

'Of course. By the way, I meant to ask. How's your move going?'

And we all know that Philippa is really asking how Kaska is feeling about breaking up from her girlfriend. It still sounds a little odd to me: *her* girlfriend.

Kaska presses the button on the remote to play 'We'll Meet Again', again. I don't know if that is ironic or tragic or just coincidence. 'It's ok, thanks. I'll be out of the flat in a few days.' This begs a lot of questions and I can see Philippa weighing up which to ask first. Before she can speak, Kaska continues, 'One of the neighbours in the block has a sofa bed. I can stay there for a few days while I find the deposit for my next place. My own place. I can't wait.'

I can't tell if the enthusiasm is sincere.

'Kind neighbour,' says Philippa.

'Yes. He is a good man. We have become friends in the last few months. We both grew up on farms. He left because he didn't like watching the cows go for slaughter after he'd worked so hard to look after them.'

'And you'll be ok sharing with a man?'

'Oh yes. It's not for long. And he knows that I ... how did he say it? Play a bat for the other side?' Kaska laughs. 'I didn't understand but he explained. And now he calls me Mrs Botham, which I don't get, but he says it kindly and with a smile. So I think maybe it's a sort of ... what was that word ... pet name?'

'Maybe. Do you trust him?'

'Oh yes. He's older, drinks raspberry tea with honey, listens to Radio 4 and has a budgie.'

This makes Philippa laugh. 'I had a budgie once. Bluey.'

'This one is green.'

'Well, as long as you trust him.'

'If there's any problem my ex will kill him. She's in the flat below.'

'I don't understand.'

'We are still friends. But nothing more, and not truly ... close, for a long time. And eventually being friends isn't enough.'

'I'm sorry,' says Philippa.

'It's ok. Besides, she was smoking too much weed. The smell makes me feel sick. I will only take a little sometimes before bed. Also, she's lovely, but she's no Sophie, so ...'

There is a pause while Philippa and I remember that Sophie is the girl Kaska left Poland with, what was it, twenty years ago?

Kaska continues, 'My new flat mate smokes much less weed. Maybe just Friday and Saturday night.'

There was a time I'd find the talk about weed unsettling, and worry about Philippa being badly influenced, but she's a fifty-nine-year-old woman so ... besides, back in the sixties, I was on Valium for a couple of years. Not that I couldn't get by without it, just that for a while, when Kenny was working a lot of overtime, Philippa was a demanding toddler, money was tight, I hated my part-time job in the baker's – I wasn't good at working out the right change for customers, I mean, twelve pennies to a shilling, twenty shillings to a pound, who thought that a good idea? – and twice a week I was taking hot dinners round to Kenny's dad while he was … ill, sort of. No wonder I was a bit down. Pat The Perm suggested I talk to the doc. He was writing out the prescription for Valium before I could sit down. I know it was prescribed, rather than illegal, but even so, I'm probably not one to judge Kaska.

I wonder if Philippa has ever taken or smoked drugs. Ciaran loved his music and took her to see The Dubliners at an open-air concert in London back in the nineties. I'm not sure she was that keen – perhaps David Essex was still her idol, haha – but Ciaran insisted, being Irish. We saw them the next day, both looking the worse for wear, but as Philippa never drank much I did wonder if they had tried something else; there was a peculiar, sickly, bitter smell to her hair, and you know what these festivals in London can be like. I think I even made a joke of it and feel sure Ciaran looked a bit guilty as he hurried outside to help Kenny with some garden digging. He was good like that. It's such a shame he and Philippa couldn't fix whatever it was that broke them.

'I hope your neighbour's sofa bed will be ok. You look tired,' says Philippa.

This is quite a bold statement from her, but true.

Kaska's reply is interrupted by Vera Lynn singing 'White Cliffs Of Dover'. Kaska looks to the TV. 'Are they really white?'

'Have you not seen them?'

'No.'

'They're sort of light grey, but then truly white if some of the cliff has fallen into the sea. The fresh chalk behind is stunning when the sun shines.'

The Michaelmas Daisy

Chapter 14
Wednesday 14th August
Hit The Road Jack

This afternoon, after finishing the ironing, putting on a second wash for damp bedding, encouraging Kenny to try some arm exercises, cleaning the patio doors – we had a such a storm a few nights ago that rain was blown fully under the patio roof and onto the glass – toileting Kenny, ringing the optician to arrange another eye test for Kenny, vacuuming the bedrooms, and giving Kenny's wheelchair and commode a good clean and antiseptic wipe-down, Philippa baked some cupcakes for tonight's art class. This evening will be her second class. She is still in the 'make a good impression' phase and I hope it works. Baking isn't really her thing, they didn't rise quite enough. Still, there's the butter icing to come, which may save the day. When Philippa was a toddler, and I baked a Victoria sponge, she was allowed to lick the spoon after I'd spread out the butter icing. Today, she takes the spoon into the lounge and gives it to Kenny who doesn't need to be asked twice.

Evening: Philippa is teaching the art class. Kaska sits with Kenny. He has no problem with that, though every time it's as if it's the first. I sit with them. She has found on YouTube a film of a train being driven though countryside, from the cab. The accompanying music is 'Hit The Road Jack'. It's on constant loop, which is soon driving me mad – I never liked the song – but suits Kenny who hums the verse and sings along to some of the chorus.

Kaska eventually joins in a couple of times until she too has had enough of the song and asks him about his work on the tracks. He remembers a little, though I wish he'd forget the grisly story of his Scottish mate, Travis, who lost a leg at the knee when he fell under a moving carriage. I met

Travis once, at a reunion do years later. He was still adamant it wasn't his fault, and made sure I knew Kenny was the first man to get to him. I joked that it had been a bugger to get the blood stain out of Kenny's work trousers – I've no idea why I thought that funny, perhaps nerves? – but they did both laugh.

When sitting with him, Kaska makes sure Kenny drinks, carefully, as swallowing seems trickier than ever for him these days, but I notice she doesn't remind him to take from the bowl of grapes at his side. I suspect the choking episode plays on her mind. It does mine. Grape skin can be a bugger.

'How was art class?' Kaska whispers. She is walking up the hall to greet Philippa, who is swapping shoes for slippers. Philippa's nose wrinkles as she sniffs deeply.

'I know,' says Kaska quietly. She closes the door to Kenny's bedroom just in case he is still awake. 'There was an accident when getting changed for bed. It's all cleared up but I didn't want to open the windows and let cold air in.'

I can't smell anything. I wonder if I've become used to the odours of various bodily functions. I'd hate to think that a visitor to our home would claim it smells like a geriatric ward. Maybe that's why Philippa has been lighting more scented candles lately.

'I'll open them tomorrow and give the house a proper airing.'

'And art class?'

'Good thanks. The cakes helped, I think. We were working on some portrait sketches. It's given me some ideas for my current piece.' She motions upstairs. 'They're a nice group and there were only three questions I couldn't answer this evening, though the answers came to me on the way home.'

'Nerves?'

'A little. Still, we had two new starters.'

'They heard about the excellent teacher, I'm sure.'

Philippa laughs.

'I better go,' says Kaska, 'my sofa bed awaits and early start in morning. The budgie hates it when I wake him up.'

Philippa thinks for a second or two before asking, 'Are you looking for a new place yet?'

'I am, but I need another hundred or so for the deposit. Nearly there.'

'Which reminds me.' Philippa finds her purse and counts out thirty-five pounds. She has agreed ten pounds an hour.

Kaska takes the money, counts it again and tries to give five pounds back.

'No, really,' says Philippa, 'I insist.'

It reminds me of Ciaran's mother. We only met his parents twice. The first was a couple of days before the wedding, and then again on the big day. The first meeting was at the working men's social club. They had come over from Dublin that day – ferry and train – and I could tell she was tired, but as we shook hands she drew to her full height – which was not a lot – gave me a warm smile and insisted her husband should buy the first round. I, of course, insisted it should be my Kenny, and there was a bit of a 'stand-off'. Ciaran's mother was not to be moved, and had that way of combining great charm with great forcefulness. But this was mother-in-law to mother-in-law, and I was not going to give way, insisting they were our guests. Fortunately, Kenny and Ciaran's dad were already laughing – politely – and Kenny said it was our pleasure to let them buy the drink, and that we would get the next two rounds. Kenny was such a diplomat. Then he ushered Ciaran's father to the bar where they took a long time to get the round and were friends by the end of the first pint of Guinness, which Ciaran's father naturally said wasn't as good as a pint from Dublin, but wasn't too bad, at which Kenny then invited himself over to Dublin in order that it could be proved.

I liked Ciaran's mum and we chatted easily all night.

She was disappointed that it wasn't a full Catholic ceremony, what with Ciaran not practicing, and happy to go with Philippa's relaxed C of E faith(ish), but I could tell her love for her son was stronger than her faith, which I think is a good thing and, to be honest, is the way I think my God would want it.

Philippa and Ciaran joined us later at the social club. It was brave, and smart, of them to let us meet each other without them. We talked about them freely before they arrived. His mother made Philippa nervous, and she could see that, so tried hard to put her at ease, and Philippa tried the same, by showing her how much she loved her son. It was touching and I was – am – so proud of her.

At the wedding, Ciaran's mother pulled me aside, between the fourth and fifth course – really, six courses in all, by which time she'd had quite a lot of wine; I guess taking sips at communion doesn't make for a tolerance – and slurred that she thought Philippa would be 'with child' by Christmas, the Martins were a fertile lot. I did wonder if there was a hint of criticism that I'd produced just the one child, but then she wouldn't have known about Sasha. As for the Martins' fertility? Turns out she got that wrong but I don't hold it against her.

We didn't get to Dublin for another ten years – Ciaran's father's funeral. It was both as sad and happy an occasion as any I can remember. I'm sorry we didn't get to know Ciaran's mother and father better, and wonder where they are now and if they are still around, somewhere, like me. If I'm still hanging around, due to God's grace, then it's the least he could do for those with such faith, isn't it? Or maybe it's the really faithful that aren't hanging around and have been allowed to move on. I wish I knew; it wouldn't change anything; I'm glad I don't.

Chapter 15
Monday 19th August
Bin And Gone

It's a Monday. The bin men are late. It doesn't matter. Kenny's an ever later riser.

'It's the bin men, Dad,' says Philippa, just as Kenny gasps when the hoist reaches that point of tension. The day's routine has already started. The only difference is that because Kenny's getting up later and later, Philippa has a chance to finish more chores between her own breakfast and getting him up. She also found half an hour to work on *that* portrait, at least I think she did, as when she came down she went straight to the bathroom to wash paint from her hands.

Kenny says nothing as she pulls down his pyjamas. His incontinence pants are not double-soiled but the pyjamas are damp so there must have been a leak. That means a bed linen change on top of everything else. Philippa looks so tired. It's 2019 for God's sake – are leakproof pants really beyond us?

'On your drive, Dad, the bin men.' Philippa tries to engage, pointing to the window.

Still, Kenny's quiet.

'Go on, tell them to be bin and gone.'

Kenny looks at her, confused.

My heart breaks again, for the first time this day, again.

At night, while Philippa sleeps, I sit with Kenny. I hear when he calls my name in the lonely, bleak hours.

Tonight he is calling more loudly than usual. His room is unlit, but some light slips past the half open door from the hall nightlight, and the curtains are not so heavy that some streetlight doesn't filter through. Neither light is enough to cause shadows beyond that which is already dark.

Kenny's awake, staring both at the ceiling and into some memory or wish. He calls my name. I'm standing over him. He calls again. Is that fear in his eyes? I can't be sure in the poor light, but pray not. He calls again. I hear Philippa stirring upstairs. It's around midnight. She's not long gone to bed. After this week's art class, when Kaska had gone, she spent time in her room. I waited outside. I think the noises I heard were of her working on that portrait.

She joins me in Kenny's room.

'Ok, Dad?'

'Beverley?'

'No, Dad, Philippa.'

'Philippa?'

'Pippa.'

'Pippa.' He smiles, then asks, 'Where's your mother?' The smile fades.

Philippa pulls a chair close, reaches over the safety bar to hold his hand, and quietly recites,

'The Michaelmas daisy grows so tall
It sees right over the garden wall,
I wonder, I wonder what it can see
For the Michaelmas daisy is taller than me.'

By the end, Kenny's smiling again and tells her, 'You're my daughter.'

Philippa nods.

'Where's Sasha?'

Of course my gasp is silent; my breath as still as ever it has been. I haven't heard the name spoken in so, so many years.

'Who's Sasha?' asks Philippa.

I don't know why I never told her. I don't know if I want Kenny to tell her now.

Then I panic that if Kenny doesn't explain, when he's gone, no one will ever know of Sasha. I pray that he tells Sasha's brief story. I hate myself for not doing it. Someone should know. Philippa must know.

'Sasha who?' asks Kenny.

The Michaelmas Daisy

Chapter 16
Saturday 24ᵗʰ August
Dark Horse

The word that springs to mind is bright; the atmosphere in the kitchen is bright, both mood and light. The backdoor's open and there is the slightest of breezes. The sun shines through the window over the sink. There is a smell of coffee and doughnuts. The coffee is instant but the doughnuts are fresh, including one with cinnamon sprinkles and a peanut butter filling – and to think I once thought pain au chocolat was exotic, haha. The doughnuts were brought by our guests. The small dining table has been pushed to one side. Philippa sits there, cradling a mug, facing Kenny who sits in his wheelchair. An old bath towel is spread out on the floor behind him. A woman, Ruby, in an orange apron and wearing blue disposable gloves, is fussing around him. Ruby has long, jet-black, straight and shiny hair, high cheekbones, an easy smile and a tall, slim figure. Actually, not so tall, just looks it for being so slim. She wields hair scissors expertly, and talks incessantly – either asking Kenny a question or answering one of her own. Holidays, pets, cars, *Eastenders*, *Hollyoaks*, favourite chocolate bars, religion, lost phone chargers, hospital visits – no topic is taboo, not even her own ex-girlfriends. Kenny's bewildered. He focuses on Philippa who offers encouraging smiles and occasionally tells him he is doing well. Ruby gives Kenny's hair a couple of squirts from a water sprayer. He flinches, even though the water is warm. She apologises, then asks if he's ever been to Southend. As it happens we have, but Kenny doesn't answer. Ruby has been there, didn't like the beach, was impressed by the length of the pier, and thought the arcades tacky but fun, though she was only twelve at the time, won a couple of quid on a flashing one-armed bandit, and the fish and chips was lovely though her aunt's had a bone

155

which nearly choked her, so, you know, swings and roundabouts, much like the funfair there.

Kenny's even more bewildered.

Ruby giggles at her own joke – she has a girlish laugh, and none the worse for that. She looks younger than Kaska. At first I thought her quickfire chatter might be down to nerves, but now I think not. I think maybe she is simply bursting with life and thoughts, and I like her.

From where Kenny sits, he can see out to the garden. Ruby remarks on how well tended it is. This isn't really true. It's all Philippa can do to keep on top of it. I certainly don't blame her.

'We don't really get to spend much time in it. Dad hasn't sat out since last summer,' says Philippa, sadly.

'Which is why I'm here,' says Raymond, the big man standing by the kettle, leaning against the worktop, trying to eat a doughnut without peanut butter dripping down his chin. He fails, but isn't embarrassed at having to roam his tongue around his lips. His tongue isn't long enough and Kaska dabs at his chin with a piece of kitchen towel. He bends a little so she can reach more. He may be a very large, hairy toddler.

I say Raymond – I notice the others always call him by the full name, never just Ray – is large, and that's true, made even more so when next to Kaska. But I don't mean he's fat. He's tall, strong looking, bit of a tummy but shoulders big enough to make it ok, a square face and few lines. He has completely grey hair but it must be long as it's pulled back into a ponytail. It suits him, which is a surprise on a man who I guess is similar in age to Philippa. He's wearing a check shirt, untucked, with the sleeves rolled up, showing hairy forearms – hairier than Kenny's. The inside of his left forearm is tattooed with a lighthouse. The red and white horizontal stripes are brightly coloured, and there's a scroll at the bottom of the tower with the inscription *'Dark Horse'*. I hope someone will ask him why. He wears what I believe are called cargo shorts these days, and has heavy legs, as hairy as his forearms. The side pocket of his shorts bulges with something. I'm not sure why, but the baggy bulge is irritating to me, though he seems a very nice man. Perhaps it's that he's just not as stylish as my Kenny.

The radio is playing Heart FM – very modern, I suppose. I've no idea what song this is but the hairdresser stops cutting for a few seconds to dance to the rhythm, singing, 'Hold my hand,' telling Philippa she, 'Loves Jess Glynne,' and asking, 'You?'

Philippa smiles. I'm pretty sure she doesn't know this singer either.

I think she's good, but no Dusty Springfield.

It's a lovely afternoon. Our kitchen feels crowded for the first time since I don't know when – maybe that Royal Jubilee in June, 2002, when we invited neighbours round for drinks. That was bold for us, and a lovely evening. Everyone enjoyed it and we all pledged to do it again but never quite got round to it.

I remember it well. Kenny and I had spent the day preparing vol au vents, sausage rolls and cheese/pineapple chunks. We'd bought in beer and wine, and thought we were all ready, when Kenny suggested maybe we should use plastic cups. By then I was in the garden, tidying the beds. They needed to look their best for our guests. I disagreed and said it was about time some of our cut glass, some of it a wedding present, saw the light. He thought it a bad idea. I thought – still think – plastic to be cheap and I wasn't going to give Pat The Perm any gossip ammunition. Kenny said I was a snob. I told him he was a philistine. He didn't know what that meant, which I said proved my point. He went down to the shed. When the first of our guests arrived, Kenny and I were still not speaking. But when Pat The Perm turned up and, in idle conversation, refused to believe the beautiful forest green shawl I wore was genuine Hermes from Paris, Kenny was there in an instant, politely putting her straight. After that we had a truly lovely evening.

Last Tuesday, as Kaska was leaving, Philippa mentioned it would be nice if they could get a proper hairdresser in to trim Kenny's hair. Philippa has been doing it for a year or two now, but it's difficult to keep tidy. It's made harder by not being a full head of hair, and a number one or two cut would look patchy. Philippa can chop it back, but there's not much style to it, and, as I say, Kenny used to be a stylish man, even in his work coverall. So a proper hairdresser – barber, I suppose – is a good idea, but getting Kenny to one is an impossibility.

'I know someone,' Kaska had said, perhaps too quickly as she added, 'but ...' and let it tail away, as if wishing she hadn't started.

'A professional who would come out?'

'Professional, no, not anymore, but very good. Used to cut my hair. Would she come out? I don't know.'

'Could you ask?'

There was some reticence on Kaska's part. Philippa didn't push and they said their goodnights. But Kaska turned at the gate and came back to Philippa at the front door, 'You know I have said it would be nice to get Kenny into the garden before the summer is over?'

Philippa nodded, a little confused, 'But I, we, can't lift the wheelchair over the patio doors and down all the steps.'

'Saturday afternoon, Kenny will have his haircut and spend an afternoon in the garden.' There was something approaching defiance in Kaska's tone.

Before Philippa could ask a question, Kaska had gone, almost skipping down the path, pleased with whatever it was she had in mind.

And so here we are. It turns out the ex-hairdresser is Kaska's ex-girlfriend, Ruby, and Raymond, the big lad, is the neighbour on whose sofa Kaska is sleeping. When Kaska first mentioned Ruby as the hairdresser, Philippa was reluctant, but Kaska was insistent.

'We are ok. We agreed I had to move out,' Kaska had told Philippa at the next respite visit. 'Ruby and me are good friends, maybe even best, and love each other, but …'

'But …'

'I don't know. Maybe it's ok to be best friends. But then stop sharing a bed.'

Philippa had sipped from her coffee, thinking that through, then asked, 'So you had to move out?'

'But Ruby's lovely. You'll see, on Saturday. And Raymond. He'll help us move Kenny into the garden.'

'Raymond?'

'The guy whose sofa I'm sleeping on. We're in the flat above Ruby's.'

This all sounds complicated to me.

Ruby finishes with an extravagant snip at a last rogue hair. Kaska taps her on the shoulder as if to compliment her on a job well done, then holds a hand mirror in front of Kenny so he can see himself.

'Is sir happy?' Ruby asks.

'You look very handsome,' Kaska tells him.

'Very,' agrees Philippa.

Kenny smiles.

'All ok?' Kaska asks him. 'Holding the rails?'

Kenny repeats the phrase back to her.

Ruby brushes stray hairs from his neck and shoulders.

'Not quite finished,' adds Raymond, dropping to his knees by the armchair to be eye level with Kenny. 'A gentleman might need his eyebrows, nose and ears trimmed. Isn't that right, sir?'

Kenny looks to Philippa who nods.

'Of course,' says Ruby, 'I rarely have to ask the ladies, except for when I do Kaska, of course.' She laughs mischievously. 'For a blonde, she is very hairy.'

'It's true,' says Raymond. 'The amount of stubble left in the plug hole after she shaves her legs in the shower …'

Kaska feigns offence.

Ruby takes a comb and scissors to Kenny's eyebrows. Kaska is still holding the mirror. Raymond remains at eye level. He has a big, unthreatening face. It's difficult to age him.

Kenny's at the centre, a race car at a pit stop surrounded by mechanics. When Ruby finishes his ears, eyebrows and nose they all take a step back. Kenny looks at Kaska, says, 'I know you,' then, to Raymond, 'Are you my brother?'

'Not quite, I'm much too big and ugly to be the brother of such a handsome young man.'

There is gentle laughter all round. Kenny doesn't understand but is happy. I stand by his side and reach to hold his hand.

'Well done, Dad, all finished,' says Philippa.

'One more thing,' says Raymond. 'When at the barber's there is one last question to ask a gentleman.'

He pauses to make sure he has all of our attention. 'I'm told sir has a reputation with the ladies. Does sir need anything for the weekend?'

Ruby whispers something to Kaska. I guess she's explaining the joke. Kaska grins and says, 'I will be jealous,' pecking Kenny on the cheek.

It's funny. Everyone laughs. I laugh more than I have in weeks, then feel humbled that these strangers should take time to brighten my Kenny's day.

I see Ruby catch Kaska's eye before asking, 'Philippa, how about you? While I have my scissors here, would you like a trim, or something bolder perhaps?'

'Yes, why not,' adds Kaska, picking up the old hairdressing magazine that is still on the kitchen table. She goes straight to the page that Philippa has been mulling over these last few months. Kaska has noticed too. It shows, to my eye, a very modern cut. A sort of unruly bob with a less than straight parting which I assume isn't a mistake. It's a style for a mature woman that suggests an intelligent and playful nature. Ok, I read that last bit in the magazine.

'That would totally suit you,' says Ruby.

'What do you think, Raymond?' Kaska asks.

'I know enough to stay on the fence when it comes to a lady's style, especially if I've only just met them. But, if pressed …'

'You are pressed,' says Ruby.

'… I'd say Philippa's hair looks lovely as it is, but would also look lovely shorter and a touch … wilder, I'm sure.'

Raymond is a charmer. Philippa's cheeks colour just a little.

'Coward,' teases Kaska.

Raymond smiles.

I think the newer style would look great on Philippa. But perhaps I still associate her longer hair with Ciaran, who I know always encouraged her to grow it.

'When the time is right, I'll have it cut,' she would say to him.

'And that'll be the right time,' he would say.

It was some kind of game they played, some kind of secret.

'Not today,' says Philippa, leaving the table to wrap up the towel on the floor so as to capture as much cut hair as possible, then pulling the Hoover from the cupboard to vacuum the strays. Raymond asks if he can have the last doughnut, though he doesn't wait for an answer. Ruby cleans her equipment and comb under the sink taps and takes great care to completely dry the stainless-steel scissors before storing them in their case. Kaska quietly watches her.

By the time the kitchen is back to normal, except for all these people, it's nearly three o'clock. Philippa passes to Kenny his Tommee Tippee cup. He takes a swallow and gives a small cough, but it passes quickly. Raymond nods at Kaska, then salutes Kenny.

'And now, MO Kenny Cooper, would you like to sit in

your garden?'

Kenny looks up from his cup and returns the salute. He doesn't answer but I can tell from the sparkle in his eyes that he'd love to. Then he says, 'Will my Beverley be there?' and looks to Philippa. She looks around the kitchen, pauses, then answers, 'Yes, Dad, in a way, Mum is there.'

I like to think she's right. The shrubs I helped to plant, the flowers I tended, the trees that Kenny trimmed under my instructions – they are all there and alive in large part because of me. So, yes, in a way, I'm there. In some way I'm there even more than I'm here.

Philippa explains to the others that she's going to get Kenny cleaned up and ready, and suggests they wait in the garden.

They have other ideas. Kaska helps with the toileting routine while Ruby and Raymond prepare a pitcher of Pimms – they have come prepared – and cut some fresh fruit into a bowl for a picnic of sorts.

Kenny's sitting in his wheelchair with clean pants, a clean shirt under a light woollen jumper, and wearing proper outdoor shoes – the first time for many months. The wheelchair is poised at the open patio doors. It needs to be manouevered over the doors' frame, down two steps onto the patio and a further three onto the garden. I watch Philippa. She has also changed, into a summer maxi dress. I haven't seen it for years, and suspect it's long out of fashion, but, being tall, the length doesn't look odd on her, and the light cotton is just right for the garden this afternoon. She's standing behind the wheelchair. Kaska and Ruby are behind her, each carrying a tray; a pitcher of Pimms, glasses and fruit snacks. Ruby has removed her apron. She wears black jeans and a black vest top but it's not dreary on her. Kaska wears light cotton dungaree shorts, plain turquoise, with a plain white t-shirt underneath. They are waiting – I don't think anyone has actually said how they are going to move

Kenny out there. There is uncertainty, until Raymond comes to the lounge – he just nipped to the loo – and pops a sliver of mango into his mouth – mango, can you believe it? I remember when bananas were exciting.

'Ready Kenny?' he asks, and bends over the wheelchair, instructing, 'Arm round my neck,' and slips one arm under Kenny's thighs and the other behind his back.

'Er, is that the plan?' Philippa asks, worry in her voice.

'It's a Nike sort of plan.' says Raymond, grinning.

'Nike?'

'Just do it.' He picks Kenny up as if a child. Kenny gives a small cry of surprise. 'Hold tight,' Raymond says to Kenny, and to Philippa, 'Do you have a garden seat or will you bring down the wheelchair. And where shall we put it?'

Before Philippa can reply, he has carried Kenny, who has put two arms around Raymond's neck, through the patio doors, and onto the patio. He turns at the top of the steps down to the garden. Kenny's smiling nervously, a little scared, a little excited. 'Oh,' says Raymond, 'Can someone grab the rug and radio I brought.'

I stand at the patio door, feeling nervous. It's a deep step down to the patio, that'll be the reason. I look behind me to the lounge. I could sit there and watch them, that would be nice, but perhaps I should, you know, take that step; after all, it's not like the patio isn't covered. It's really just another part of the house.

In the garden they are choosing a spot on the grass, at the bottom of the garden, in the shade of the old apple tree. Philippa places a foldup garden chair. Raymond carefully lowers Kenny into it. It's rickety and I worry it will topple. Kaska lays out the blanket, Ruby looks after the Pimms and fruit. Raymond switches on the transistor radio. Dionne Warwick is singing 'Do You Know The Way To San Jose?'

Standing at the patio door, I sing along. Kenny looks a little uncomfortable but not fearful. Philippa, sitting on the grass next to him, reaches up to hold his hand. Kaska pours drinks.

I watch, and feelings of intense loneliness weigh on me, but also draw me forward. I step as lightly as I can on the first step, then the second, on the patio but still under cover. It's nice here, the air is fresh but it's just like being indoors, isn't it?

Philippa hands a glass of Pimms to Kenny, with no fruit. He cradles the cup in one hand and supports the base with the other, as if worried about the glass's fragility.

When everyone has a glass, Raymond raises his, 'To Kenny.'

'To Kenny,' they repeat, even Kenny. He sips, coughs a little, then sips some more. Unprompted, he recites,

'The Michaelmas daisy grows so tall
It sees right over the garden wall,
I wonder, I wonder what it can see
For the Michaelmas daisy is taller than me.'

His voice is gentle and melodic. The audience applauds gently. We hear Shogun bark. Raymond says something to Kenny who repeats the poem and I think Raymond is trying to learn it.

From up here on the patio I can't catch all that is being said. I am desperate to hear more, to be with them. I despair that I might be forever lonely if I'm not there, with Kenny, or Philippa. I take the few steps down to the lawn and edge closer to them. The sun is warm, I imagine, and I tell myself to enjoy this freedom, though my heart is pounding – how is that possible? Get a grip, Beverley.

Raymond is talking to Kenny. Philippa chips in occasionally. Kenny looks settled, if a little unsupported in the garden chair.

Kaska and Ruby are talking. About what, I have no idea. Kaska takes Ruby's hand, kisses the palm then presses it gently back into Ruby's lap.

Philippa passes round the fruit snacks. Kaska refills glasses, Raymond stands to act out some story he is telling. Kenny watches Raymond, transfixed by his flailing arms and legs, and laughs when the others do. I remember again those summer park entertainers of Philippa's childhood.

Raymond sits back on the rug and pulls a battered tobacco tin, Golden Virginia, and lighter from his cargo shorts pocket. He goes to light what looks like a roll-up from here but I notice Kaska gently nudge him. He shrugs and puts it away. Instead, from the same pocket, he pulls one of those electronic cigarette things I've seen on the TV. A few seconds later there is a hint of berries in the air.

Next door, Shogun barks again.

Raymond fiddles with the transistor radio volume. 'Whiter Shade Of Pale' is playing.

The air is still, the insect buzz is more a feeling than a sound, perhaps a memory, and the birdsong is just as when I was a child. I cry gentle, and welcome, tears for my own parents, and smile easily with the memory of the joy we shared when I was a child.

This has been a good garden, a giving garden. There was a time I'd sit and imagine Sasha running round, chasing a pet dog or rabbit or pedalling furiously on a tricycle or playing chase with friends before a picnic of jam sandwiches and cream soda. There was a time I imagined Philippa and Ciaran's children – it was always plural – doing the same. Kenny pushing them in a wheelbarrow, playing football with them, teaching them cricket while Philippa and Ciaran looked on, proud.

Eventually, Kenny falls asleep. Raymond carries him back to the lounge. I follow, eager and, I admit, relieved to be back indoors. Raymond gently places him in the riser/recliner. Philippa drapes a blanket over his lap.

'Ok to make coffee?' asks Raymond, going through to the kitchen.

'Of course,' says Philippa, following.

They watch Kaska and Ruby through the kitchen window while waiting for the kettle to boil. I sense that Philippa wants to ask Raymond about the girls' relationship, I know I do. Instead she indicates to Raymond's tattoo and, specifically. the script underneath, 'Why dark horse?'

Raymond looks down at the image, almost as if reminding himself. 'I'm a big George Harrison fan, and I love lighthouses.'

'George Harrison?'

'It was his nickname.'

'Lighthouse?'

Raymond laughs; a full belly-laugh. 'Dark horse.'

'Oh,' says Philippa. I think this makes as little sense to her as it does me.

'A story for another time,' says Raymond as the kettle boils.

Sunday. The house is quiet. Kenny's in the lounge. The TV is on: *Bargain Hunt*. I'm in the kitchen with Philippa. Yesterday was a lovely day for us all. Today, Philippa has so far ignored the chores apart from getting Kenny ready for the day and feeding him – which is a day's work in itself, and I notice Kenny's stubble looks patchy. I think sometimes he insists on shaving himself, stubborn as a daisy.

The kitchen is yet to be cleared. The washing machine is not loaded, the recycling not taken out to the blue bin, and the microwave not wiped down following yesterday evening's mishap when reheating a cup of coffee. Instead, Philippa is going through bank statements – hers and Kenny's – and re-reading the letter from Social Services about Kenny's respite funding.

Yesterday feels a long time ago. There is a sound from the front garden. Philippa looks up to see if there is someone at the door. There isn't. She looks disappointed and goes into the lounge. Kenny's now sleeping. She looks at the small denim jacket draped over the dining chair. It's Kaska's, left the previous day.

Yesterday was a good day.

Today will be a long day.

The Michaelmas Daisy

Chapter 17
Wednesday 28th August
Sasha

Kenny looks agitated and afraid. His eyes follow Kaska. She looks worried. I feel a rising sense of panic. It has been nearly five minutes. He looks around, for Philippa I suppose, but she's at the community centre, teaching the art class.

Kaska had gently convinced Kenny it was time to get ready for bed. The hoist was dragged into place, Kenny's position prepared, the sling connected. Kaska pressed the button. The hoist began its pull, Kenny gasped at the point of tension, of course, and Kaska reassured him. The hoist lifted him from the chair, and though his feet touched the base plate they took almost none of his weight. Just as he was close to full height the whirring motors slowed, and died. The hoist stopped.

Kenny is suspended.

That was five minutes ago. Nothing has changed.

Kaska removes the battery again. It had a full set of lights earlier, Philippa always has it charged. Now the lights are dark. Kaska clicks it back into its compartment and presses the button, again. Nothing happens. She looks around the room. I don't know why.

'Ok, Kenny?' she asks.

Kenny forces a smile, then winces. I guess the sling is starting to bite into the flesh under his arms. It's taking most of his weight, slight as that has become.

Kaska retains her smile but I can see the concentration

169

in her eyes, hunting for a solution. She can't unclip the sling. Kenny would drop like a stone and, now being suspended a few inches away from the chair, as well as above it, there's no guarantee he wouldn't collapse to the floor. Even if he isn't injured, Kaska could not lift him from there, and the stuck hoist will be no use. She looks round the room, again. She stands close to Kenny, tests the length of her arms with one behind him and the other stretching for the sling hook over the hoist. She cannot reach, but even if she could, it would mean having to somehow lift Kenny sufficiently to take the tension off the hook. That is not going to happen.

Kenny's smile fades. He winces and mutters something. I don't think he's angry. He's distressed. Apart from the pain of suspension, he's scared, doesn't understand, and doesn't know what question to ask of Kaska.

There is a quiet moan of pain.

I, too, now feel fear. I pray Kenny won't call my name, expecting me to be there to help. How many more times must I fail him?

Kaska needs to sort this out. She apologises to Kenny, scrabbles in her bag for her phone, to ring Philippa, I guess, but she rings Raymond.

I hear her side of the conversation: firm; clear; no nonsense. I'm sure Raymond will be on his way. I hope he's nearer than Philippa, who I expect Kaska to ring next. She doesn't.

Kenny releases his grip of the hoist handle and slips an inch or two. Is it possible for him to drop through the sling somehow? I didn't think the hand grip did anything, but perhaps it kept his shoulders wide enough for the sling to stay in place under his arms. He slips another inch.

'Kaska!' I scream. 'Kaska!'

Kaska sees, turns and leaves the room.

'Kaska!' I scream again, to her back, though I don't believe she's running away. But screaming is all I have.

She returns in seconds, having gone to leave the front

door open. She slips behind Kenny, sitting on the chair, knees close to the back of Kenny's legs. If he slips through the sling there's a good chance he will be in her lap. But she is so tiny. Kenny slips again with a gasp of pain and surprise. The sling must be cutting into skin. Kaska leans forward and tries to take some of the weight from him, singing, 'Kiss Me Goodnight Sergeant Major'. Kenny does not join in.

Three minutes pass.

Kenny slips further.

Five more minutes pass

If Kenny goes all the way and his weight topples forward a little, I fear Kaska may not catch him on her lap.

Four more minutes pass.

Kaska sings, 'Knees Up Mother Brown', a little breathlessly. Trying to take some of Kenny's weight is tiring her.

Kenny slips again.

Kaska tries 'Those Were The Days My Friend.'

Kenny grimaces, in pain.

'… we thought they'd never …' A deep voice joins Kaska's as Raymond comes into the lounge, moving quickly but not in a panic. 'Hello, Kenny. Bit of a pickle there?' His smile is falsely broad. 'Swap,' he says to Kaska.

She slips out from behind Kenny, Raymond squeezes his way in, just. He has to put his arms around Kenny's chest to lift and move him away from the chair so that he, himself, can get fully behind. It works well and I can see he now takes all of Kenny's weight from the sling.

Kenny still looks scared and his confusion grows.

Kaska can now release the sling from its hooks. Raymond drops back into the riser/recliner with Kenny in his lap, singing, 'We thought they'd never end.' Kenny joins in but with neither relief nor joy.

When Philippa comes home, Kaska has just got Kenny to bed. She's sitting in the kitchen with Raymond, drinking tea.

Philippa is surprised to see Raymond, who is about to speak but is interrupted by Kaska.

'I needed Raymond's help, with Kenny.'

Kaska explains, formally, clearly, leaving out nothing, what happened to Kenny. By the end, she's swallowing tears. Raymond is playing it down and goes to put an arm around her, but Kaska shrugs him off, making sure Philippa realises the seriousness of the incident.

'It's ok,' says Raymond, 'Kenny's only light and I was here.'

'You were not,' says Kaska. 'I rang you to come.'

'Yeah, but it's ten minutes away and …' Raymond starts, but Kaska's expression silences him.

Philippa watches and listens. I hope she realises Kaska is right to be so serious.

'I'm sorry,' says Kaska, 'I thought the battery was charged.' There is a catch in her voice.

'It was, fully,' says Philippa. 'There must be something wrong with it. Not your fault.'

'I should have checked.'

'How? If anything, I'm to blame. There's a spare battery I keep charged. I haven't told you where it is. That's my fault. Not yours.'

'There is no fault,' says Raymond.

'You should have rung me though,' says Philippa.

Before Kaska can speak, Raymond motions Philippa to sit with them at the table and rests a big hand gently on her forearm. 'I'm closer than the community centre. It made sense. And all's well that ends well.'

I don't know what to make of what happened. I have calmed down; we all have; the first to settle was Kenny. I don't want Kaska to feel guilty, nor Philippa. Yet I feel shame. I was, again, bloody useless, but more than that, I have the nagging feeling that if only Sasha were around everything would be different. He would be sharing this with Philippa. He would have been there to help her and Kenny when I fell ill. He would have been able to help them both through my cremation, help them grieve, help Kenny keep on top of the house as he got older. He would have supported Philippa through her divorce, maybe even have spoken to Ciaran about it, was it for the best? I don't know, might Sasha have stopped it? Might Sasha have had a family of his own? Grandchildren to help with checking on Kenny and caring. Sasha might have been good at dealing with the hospital and Social Services. I'm sure he would have been. And tonight, when Kenny needed help, he might have been here, or, at least, round the corner.

And I know all those reasons are no reasons at all for having a child. I would not wish any of those responsibilities on him. But still, he wasn't there when Kenny needed him and I can't help but feel it's my fault; after all these years, still guilty.

And I don't wish any of those responsibilities on Philippa either. So guilty.

Back in the kitchen, it's just Philippa, Kaska and me. Raymond left a little while ago, sensing the girls wanting to be alone, I think.

'He seems a nice guy. And has a budgie,' says Philippa, unnecessarily filling the silence.

'Yep. If I wasn't gay I probably wouldn't stay on the sofa.' Kaska smiles; first time since Philippa came home.

'How old is he?' Philippa asks, overly casual.

'Getting on for sixty I think. He's sort of retired. I hoped you two would get on.'

'Quite a bit older than you then, if you were, you know, to leave the sofa.' Philippa teases.

'Oh, I wouldn't mind that. After all I am twelve years older than Ruby,' Kaska says, but her smile dies, 'though I guess in the end that's why I'm on the sofa.'

Philippa waits.

'I'm not what Ruby needs. She should be out living. I want quiet nights in. And it became too … convenient.'

'But I saw, on Saturday, you two are so close.'

'Maybe, but sometimes it's too easy to stop living the difference between friend and lover.' Kaska looks up from her mug of tea. 'But it's ok, Raymond's sofa is very comfy.'

Philippa nods, as if understanding, which I'm not sure I do, and says, hesitatingly, 'I … I've got a spare room upstairs.'

'No, I couldn't, but thank you.'

'Think about it.'

It's close to half eleven by the time Kaska leaves. Philippa waves to her from the door then checks on Kenny. Though it's dark, we can see his eyes are open. They are wet.

'Ok, Dad? Sounds like you had quite an evening.'

'Beverley?'

'Philippa. Pippa.'

Kenny raises a hand. Philippa takes it. Kenny squeezes tight.

Chapter 18
Friday 30th August
Abide With Me

The stroke, if that's what it was, might have happened just as *News At Ten* started, yesterday night. It had been a pleasant evening. Philippa had flicked through YouTube on the TV to find some hymns – 'Abide With Me' was the favourite – that had sub-titles, then found some old episodes of *Dad's Army*. Kenny didn't follow them but some memories may have been triggered, and he smiled along with the audience laughter. As the news started, Philippa brought in the hoist, it was time to get Kenny ready for bed. The riser/recliner was raised and Philippa went to place the sling around Kenny's back, but he slumped to the left, eyes glazing over. He didn't answer Philippa's questions and slipped down a little further, staring at the fireplace. Some spittle dribbled from the side of his mouth.

Philippa reclined the chair so that gravity pulled him to lie back more centrally, and tried to gain his attention. She stayed calm. I didn't. I think we both assumed a stroke or a fit, and he didn't react to my screaming his name – and yes, I know that joke stopped being funny long ago.

Philippa took a few deep breaths and rang for an ambulance, then Kaska. She, and Raymond, arrived in less than a quarter of an hour. When he heard that the ambulance was likely to be another forty minutes he suggested, gently, to Philippa that, 'We don't have to wait.' She understood and nodded. Raymond picked Kenny out of the chair, asking for a blanket to keep him warm in the car. Philippa and Kaska went into Kenny's bedroom to sort out contents for an overnight bag. I stood at the open front door. The night outside looked cold, though of course I couldn't feel it. The darkness, instead of closing the night in, was vast beyond the streetlights, vast enough to be everywhere all at once despite its emptiness, an emptiness that pressed in on me. Raymond loaded Kenny into his Volvo's front seat. I took the small step out onto the porch then froze, scared into inaction and lack of decision. Last Saturday, time outside in the garden, in the sunshine, had been almost exciting, but had not prepared me for leaving the house, my house, my home, at night. Raymond started the car and was waiting patiently when Kaska joined him. Philippa closed the front door behind me and I started at the slam. The night was darker still. Philippa double-locked the door with trembling hands, matching my own. She needed me. Kenny needed me, out there. I followed her to the car, head down, pretending the night didn't exist, repeating a mantra, 'Kenny, Kenny, Kenny, Kenny …'

We were at A & E in ten minutes where my panic burst free – panic driven by fear of being so far from home, and terror at Kenny's deterioration.

A & E was packed; there was no one to hear me.

Philippa found the resolve to slowly and precisely describe Kenny's symptoms to a nurse. I grasped at, and fed from, her exaggerated calm. Kenny was seen quickly and when it was obvious that he should be kept in, Philippa insisted Raymond and Kaska go home. Raymond agreed, on condition that when Philippa finally needed a lift, she ring him, no matter the time. I didn't want them to go. There being just Philippa and me didn't feel enough.

I returned to my mantra occasionally through the night, but ever more slowly until it was for Kenny's sake rather than mine.

'Why …'

Kenny's faltering mumble drags me from my daydream – about what I have no idea; my mind has been rambling – and I feel guilty that I wasn't paying attention. We have been here hours, long enough that my 'Kenny' mantra is no longer a comfort; last night's fear has bedded down into a constant unease.

Kenny's eyes search his surroundings. I lean close to his face, trying to speak the words for him, though I don't know what he wants to say.

'Why … am I … here?' he finally asks. It has taken a much concentration to say those four words. They are little more than a whisper. He looks exhausted, with eyes half-closed. Fresh white pillows exaggerate his pallor.

I feel a sudden fear, a new one, another one. Though Kenny is but inches away, he looks detached, like a subject in a tableau: *'The Model Patient'*. White sheets, with a blue blanket, are tucked neatly to his chest. His arms are on top of the covers and he wears a clean ward gown. Into the back of his left hand is a cannula, fed from a saline drip hanging at the bed's side. The vein is raised where the needle intrudes and bruising blooms already. There is an oxygen sensor on his right forefinger and a blood pressure wrap on his upper arm. The machine beside him blinks steadily, the numbers look ok, I suppose; there are no nurses or doctors fussing around him. The bedhead is raised, perhaps forty-five degrees. The bed rails are set, even though he's incapable of going anywhere. There is a tube running from under the covers into the bag hanging from the bed frame, collecting urine via a catheter. The urine is dark yellow in colour. There is no smell.

No, wait, not a subject in a tableau, he's more two dimensional than three; more like a figure in a painting or a photograph in a glossy medical procedure book. He has been sanitised. I look to Philippa, about to decry what they've done to him, then remember I can't, but she looks my way and it makes me wonder, again.

His name is written on a board on the wall behind the bed. The writing is clear but not as neat as I would like:

Kenneth Alfred Cooper. D.O.B. 9/10/31.

'Why am I still here?' Kenny mumbles again.
Philippa stands from the chair by the bed and removes

her cardigan. I guess it's warm in this ward, much warmer than the corridor in which we spent much of last night and most of the morning. There is a wheeled table at the bed's end. She pours some cold water from the plastic jug into a plastic cup and offers it to Kenny, tilting it just enough to provide the merest of sips. Kenny holds it in his mouth until Philippa suggests he swallows.

The curtains have been pulled around the bed. It's early evening. The ward lights are bright. Once an hour, give or take, a nurse slips behind the curtain to write numbers from the monitor screen next to the bed onto a chart. The nurse asks Philippa how she is and if there's anything she wants. I think Philippa's tired and scared and wants a doctor to tell her exactly what's happened, and what they are doing about it, but she tells the nurse she is fine. The nurse looks apologetic, I don't know why, and leaves.

'Why am I here? B ... Bev ... Bevevie?' Kenny stumbles over my name.

'They think you've had a stroke, Dad,' says Philippa.

But I know that's not the answer to the question he's asking.

Visiting time will end soon: 9pm. We have been here nearly twenty-four hours. I hate it. There are so many people, so much noise, even when no one is around and nothing is happening. I don't want to be here. I feel sick. I feel trapped and cling to Kenny's side. It was hard to leave the house, but how could I not? It may be harder to leave here. I'm scared. I fear the time is coming when I may need to make real choices, hard decisions – first time in years; since I was alive, perhaps.

Raymond and Kaska are waiting in the pickup area. Philippa gives them an update but they drive mostly in silence. They both see Philippa into our house and Kaska puts on the kettle. I am glad to be back. I am distraught that Kenny's not with us and fret as to whether I should be with him.

Who needs me more? Am I foremost a mother, or a wife? I don't know, but Philippa looks exhausted and I can't bear the thought that she will be in the house on her own if I stay at the hospital. She has not cried since she came home. I think she's in shock. After a mug of tea, Raymond says his goodbyes, emphasising that he's around to run Philippa to the hospital and back any time, and offering to pick up shopping and help with chores. He's softly spoken for a big lad, and his quiet words carry authority and sincerity. He pecks her on the cheek to make sure, I think, she knows he means it when he tells her not to forget to look after herself.

He shows himself to the door. Kaska doesn't follow. Philippa's look is quizzical. Kaska says, 'I thought I'd try your sofa, for a few nights, if that's ok. And I will pay rent, so if you wanted to make up a bed in the spare room, that would be even better.'

Philippa leaves her chair to hug her.

It's cruel beyond words that I cannot hold my daughter, or be held. It's more cruel still to watch someone else comfort her. I feel rising resentment and then shame at such selfishness.

Later, I stand on the landing, listening to the steady breathing coming from Kaska in the spare room, and watching the sliver of light at the crack of the closed door to Philippa's. Occasionally, a shadow passes across the light; Philippa is not yet in bed. I won't go in, but I am here, still.

The Michaelmas Daisy

Chapter 19
Tuesday 3rd September
Those Were The Days My Friend

It's Kenny's fourth full day on the ward. Philippa and I have been here every day, often brought and picked up by Raymond – he insisted, in a gentle way. Philippa insisted, also gently, on paying for petrol and parking, and, after a polite degree of protest, he took a fiver so she could keep her pride; he found the right balance, I think.

On the first day after Kenny's admission, Philippa woke early. I was already awake – of course – and waiting for her in the kitchen. Kaska soon joined us. It was the strangest morning we've had since Philippa came back home. It was the slowest and the quietest, despite Kaska's presence. It was in no way relaxing as we all watched the clock, anxious to be ringing the ward to see how Kenny was and to ask when we could visit.

Philippa rang at just past nine, to be told that Kenny was, 'Comfortable,' had had a, 'Comfortable night,' and was looking forward to a, 'Comfortable day,' whatever that might mean. A nurse had said something similar to me when I'd rung after Kenny had been taken in with appendicitis all those years ago. I didn't believe her; I had been with Kenny when they took him in, and 'comfortable' was not the word to describe Kenny thrashing in agony, strapped on a silly little stretcher, crowded into a cold ambulance, a young nurse sitting at his side, smiling falsely. I'd been scared and wasn't again comfortable until he came home.

I'm scared now. Scared that Kenny won't come home. Scared that he's in pain, alone, cold and calling for help that doesn't come.

I'm also scared to be leaving the house again, but there is no choice, and I'm ashamed to feel such fear when so much now rests on Philippa's shoulders.

181

I came home with Philippa on the first and second evenings, torn between staying with Kenny and keeping Philippa company. I opted, after painful consideration, for Philippa, even though Kaska stayed with us, but last night I stayed on the ward, with Kenny. A ward at night is the saddest place in the world, and I wished Kenny had slept through, but he woke often, each time with fear in his eyes. I reminded him of that first night we spent under the same roof, when Kenny learnt my dad could snore and pass wind simultaneously, and then, months later, the first time we slept under the same covers – though we didn't sleep much. Kenny had been invited to a cousin's wedding, near Croydon. His uncle offered to put us up for the night and I swore to my mum we'd have separate rooms. We did, but I didn't stay in mine. Were Kenny's uncle and aunt hard of hearing? Heavy sleepers? Had the Babycham and stout Kenny had been buying them all evening the desired effect? Or did they simply turn a blind eye? Doesn't matter, it was, of course, an unforgettable night. Did we get it right? Not first time. Not second. At least I don't think so as it was uncomfortable, not as much as the girls on the fish stall teased me it would be – I worked Saturdays at the market for a while; hated it – but those first couple of times hurt. I tried not to show the pain, but he saw, and heard, and stopped. He was mortified, embarrassed and disappointed he hadn't 'got it right', and worried he'd not put the rubber on properly. So many feelings for the poor man to manage. I told him, in a whisper, it was all right and I didn't mind, and that we'd try again in a few minutes. We'd find out together. And I don't know if we ever 'got it right', but we learnt how to make it right for each other. It took longer than it probably should as it was awkward to talk about 'it'. Never mind that no one had ever told us anything about 'it', no one had told us how to talk about 'it' without embarrassment or foolish giggles. But we found our way, and found our own expressions, hence I always smiled and blushed when Kenny mentioned rhubarb and custard, even in innocence.

Sometimes I feel I may never smile again.

So, day four, and here we are, in a room just down the corridor from the nurses' station. It's cluttered with shelving, holding haphazard collections of files and books. There's a kettle and some mugs on a small table. The mugs have not been washed and there are round coffee stains on the table's top. There are five of us. In a half-circle sit Philippa, Raymond, Nurse Clodagh and Doctor something – he spoke quickly and I didn't catch his name. We've been here a good few minutes, waiting for two more people – someone from Social Services and someone from an NHS Social Care Department, the name of which is very long and said to us in such a way as to make me think they don't want us to remember it in case we try to make contact in the future. Cynical? They make it hard not to be. And the room smells of eggs.

The hospital had rung Philippa that morning, asking her to come in, but stressing it wasn't because of a change in Kenny's condition. I was annoyed that they felt they had to summon her; she would be coming up anyway, they should know that by now. Raymond brought her and is with us, waiting patiently, with no small-talk.

The Social Services and Social Care Stupidly Long Name Department people enter. One's a lady, one's a man – though I didn't catch who came from which department, and the badges hanging from their necks have such small photos and writing that I can't make them out. I can't even be sure the photo is of them.

They take the two empty seats. The room is crowded, but there is silence, and I wonder if they are waiting for Philippa to do something. Eventually, the nurse suggests they run round the room doing introductions again – what a waste of time – and each explains why they are there in jargon that I can't follow. Finally, the NHS – or Social Services – lady asks,

'So, Philippa, how do you think your father is doing?' She speaks softly, trying hard to be empathetic, but sounding patronising. My cynicism deepens daily.

Philippa looks confused. 'How do *I* think he's doing?'

'Yes.' The woman leans forward in the chair and clasps her hands together, as if in prayer.

Philippa looks at Raymond. He seems to understand her quizzical look.

'Surely, one of you should be telling Philippa,' he says, in his gentle but convincing tones.

The woman sits back, smiles and looks to the doctor. I can't tell if it's a smile of agreement, condescension or defiance.

'Mr Cooper's had a stroke. He's doing well,' says the doctor.

'And do you think he'll get better?' the man from either Social Services or NHS Social Care asks.

Philippa, Raymond and I wait, assuming the question to be for the doctor. The doctor leans forward and looks at Philippa.

Eventually Raymond says, his voice just a touch louder, but still calm, though with a hint of criticism, 'You're expecting Philippa to answer that, too?'

Now it's the nurse's turn to smile benevolently and lean forward. 'And what if Mr Cooper doesn't?' she asks.

'Doesn't what?' Philippa asks.

'Get better,' says the doctor.

'He'll need a great deal of support,' says the man.

'He has dysphagia,' adds the doctor.

Philippa waits for someone to explain what that means. So do I, and I've watched my fair share of *Casualty* over the years.

The doctor feels obliged to fill the silence. 'And when he's fully dysphagic? Well then, I'm afraid …'

More silence, until Raymond speaks, his voice a little louder again. 'You may think you're explaining something, but you're really not.'

'It's about understanding the nature of the progression of the condition and …' says the NHS man.

'Enough.' says Philippa. 'Someone needs to speak plainly.' Her tone dares anyone not to. Raymond nods agreement.

Without looking into her face, the doctor says that dysphagia means swallowing difficulties, and when Kenny can no longer take food by mouth, the symptoms of Kenny's stroke, and his age, means that they would not consider feeding through other ways; no more tubes. In short, he would be on an 'end of life pathway'. It takes a second for the words to register, then I feel the floor give way under my feet, somehow. Ridiculously, I grasp at a table for support.

Philippa swallows hard – which is ironic, I suppose – and asks, 'How long?'

'We don't know,' says someone.

Philippa takes a deep breath. 'Meantime?'

'There's not much more to be done on the ward,' says the doctor.

I feel faint.

'Though we keep him comfortable,' the Nurse Clodagh chips in, feeling the need to defend 'the ward'.

'Here, these may help,' says the woman, passing a thin sheaf of A4 papers stapled to form a short booklet. They are poor photocopies. The first page is titled: 'Nursing Home, Care Home or Home Care – What You Need To Know.'

There is a list of contents under the title. I notice Chapter One is 'Payment Options'.

They go through the papers with Philippa, but the rest of the meeting is a blur. I hope Philippa and Raymond are taking it in, but Philippa's eyes are teary and far-staring, so I guess not.

We are back at Kenny's bedside. The cannula is still in his hand but there are no lines attached. He no longer has a blood pressure wrap on his arm, and has more colour, sitting up, bolstered by a bunching of pillows. He looks anxious as we slip in through a gap in the curtains. Philippa switches on her smile. Kenny tries to match it, saying, 'I ... know ...' but he doesn't finish. It's hard to form words, for all of us.

Raymond salutes and asks, 'Holding the rails, MO Kenny?'

Kenny's smile broadens and he mutters something. I think he's repeating, 'Holding the rails.' His speech is worse than yesterday. He holds out a hand to Philippa.

My heart breaks. Again. Again. Into how many more pieces can a broken heart be fractured?

Raymond softly sings, 'Those Were The Days My Friend.'

We have been here nearly twenty minutes. Philippa and Raymond sit one side of Kenny's bed. I sit on the other. I am holding Kenny's hand and swear I can feel the warmth.

Don't dare tell me I can't. Don't you bloody dare.

Philippa has been flicking through the papers she has been given. No one has tried to give Kenny a sip of orange squash and I think it's because we're terrified today may be the day he can no longer swallow.

'I'll take him home. I can manage,' says Philippa, handing the papers to Raymond as if they are not needed; decision made.

Raymond nods but says, 'It's a two-person job now. All the time. After the stroke, Kenny has no mobility at all.'

'Which makes it even easier, surely? It's not like he's going to run off.' There is no humour in her tone.

'He'll need bed-baths, turning, feeding by hand ...'

'Not so different from now.'

'And a proper full cradle hoist. Have you room?'

'He's not going into a nursing home. He's coming home to … to die.'

Her voice drifts away in a tremble, and she looks at Raymond. He reaches out a big arm. She shuffles her chair closer to him and buries her head in the crook of his neck and shoulder. His arms wrap around her, as if she is a child.

She sobs quietly and whispers, 'If Dad doesn't come home, what am I for?'

I, too, sob, despairingly, and alone.

We spend another ten or fifteen minutes. Raymond goes for coffee. Kenny stirs and Philippa touches his arm. He opens his eyes but doesn't return Philippa's smile.

'Bevervy, why … here?' he whispers, with effort.

And I think of the alternative.

A month or so before I died, when it hurt beyond the painkiller's reach, in the early hours I'd turned in bed to face him, touched his shoulder so he too would turn – I knew he was still awake. I'd prepared a little speech, ending with the suggestion that now was the time, except, rather than stick with our agreement of so many years, there was no need for both of us to go, only me, and I knew he was brave enough to go through with it.

But I'd said nothing.

We had looked at each other, with just enough illumination from the nightlight to see each other's tears.

But I'd said nothing.

He was already burdened with guilt, whatever happened. Who was I to add more?

The Michaelmas Daisy

Chapter 20
Wednesday 18th September
Bitter

The discussion with the Social Services and NHS Social Care Department that cannot be named was two weeks ago. Afterwards, Raymond dropped Philippa home. I went with them, wanting to know Philippa's thoughts, but guilt-ridden at leaving Kenny. Raymond hinted that he could come in for tea if she wanted to chat, but she hinted even more strongly that she would prefer to be alone. As far as I could tell, that night she didn't sleep. She tried watching TV, then reading – *The Thorn Birds*, still – then made a pot of tea. She got ready for bed but didn't stay in her room long and joined me in Kenny's bedroom, in the dark. It was a long night.

It's been a long fortnight. The thin sheaf of notes outlining Kenny's – Philippa's? – options lies on the kitchen table, increasingly dog-eared, tatty and covered with scribbled thoughts as Philippa goes through it at least four times a day; sometimes alone, sometimes with Kaska, always with me, always with emotions bouncing between guilt and … and what? Relief? Resignation? Resolve? My own opinion changes daily, almost as often as Philippa's.

Philippa has looked at four nursing homes – care homes cannot provide for Kenny. I don't go with her. I am getting better at being with whichever of them I choose, and the house is no prison, so I often stay with Kenny at the hospital. He receives, I suppose, adequate attention: changing him; changing sheets; bed washing; feeding – unenthusiastically; turning. But there is little or no conversation – too busy I suppose – and no stimulation. There is much talk about discharging him.

I try to be back with Philippa when she returns from

visiting potential nursing homes. She has a routine. She walks in slowly, makes a cup of tea, sits at the kitchen table and tries not to cry. She picks up the brochure the home has given her and flicks through it. Then she searches the internet for, I guess, some new, elusive nursing home which ticks all the items on her list, and has that magic X factor that screams it's exactly the right one for Kenny – for without that, how can she know?

I think that place probably does not exist.

I want her to bring Kenny home. Then I worry about how much work it would be and want her to choose a nursing home. Then I fear for Kenny being alone in the nursing home and want him here. Then I brood over Philippa not living the life she should.

How cruel for Philippa to have to decide.

This evening, Philippa is with Kaska and Raymond, talking. They listen. Philippa cries some more. They wait. Eventually, well into the night by now, Kaska talks of Kenny's needs and comfort, and our inability to change anything. The best we can do for Kenny is to bring him a smile and a song and to sit and hold his hand and let him know he's loved. And, if a nursing home looks after the practical stuff, Philippa would have the time and energy to bring that smile and song. It's time for another way.

Raymond says little. Philippa looks to him, wondering.

'At times like these,' says Raymond, 'I ask myself what would George Harrison say?'

'Who?' asks Kaska.

Raymond smiles; a gentle, dark horse smile. 'Sometimes there can be more peace than guilt in accepting the inevitable.'

Chapter 21
Wednesday 25ᵗʰ September
Hope

Kenny has been in the nursing home for nearly a week already. Oak Meadows is an old manor house, converted and extended. Some of the older parts have woodchip wallpaper that looks to be coated in at least five layers of magnolia emulsion. The newer parts are more clinical, but the main lounge smells of cabbage, though I have never seen it on the menu.

Oak Meadows was chosen not because it ticked more boxes than the others – they were all suitable according to brochures and inspection reports – but because Philippa's instinct drew her to Liliya, the manageress. Of course, at other times, her instinct told her to bring Kenny home. The decision was a painful see-saw – tears of abandonment and fear of poor care at one end, fear of not coping and tears of exhaustion at the other.

Either way – fears and tears. The loneliest decision Philippa has ever made.

Perhaps Raymond's advice, courtesy of George Harrison, the dark horse, tipped the see-saw.

Liliya's smile, sincere and empathetic, tipped it further; reasons as good as any, according to Kaska. She trusts her instincts, which is a useful trait to have, I suppose. I'm not sure I ever had that. I don't know about Philippa. And I'm not so sure Kaska is right in this instance, but the hospital was pressing for Kenny to be discharged and, in truth, apart from the auxiliary staff, few of the nurses in hospital had time to talk to Kenny or feed him properly. I don't blame them, they are so busy, but of course I resent it. Caring for the infirm is their job.

Anyway, it was time to take Kenny away from there. So, Oak Meadows it is, at least for now, Philippa tells Kaska, and I want to believe that, but …

Social Services were quick to agree. They were even quicker to make sure Philippa filled out all the forms showing how much Kenny has in the bank. Social Services and the NHS will pay towards the nursing costs, but because we have some savings above twenty-three thousand or so – amazing to think we managed to put aside such a huge sum, disappointing we never took that cruise – Kenny will have to fork out for the accommodation and living costs. And they were quick to pass Philippa the papers detailing how they'll put something called a charge on the house. If Kenny's there a long time and his savings run out – which won't take long at a thousand a week – a week! – they'll get their money when the house is sold. I try not to be bitter. Besides, will he live long? Some days, when I can be strong, I think not, and, meanwhile, for Kenny to be properly looked after will be a good use for our money.

Would I want to live at Oak Meadows? Probably not. More importantly, would I settle for dying there?

Sometimes, while Kenny's napping, I have a mooch. Most of the residents are mobile, some are in wheelchairs. I assume that a few, like Kenny, are confined to bed as I see staff wander in and out of bedrooms, but no patients ever emerge. The residents are a mixed bunch, as are the staff, but they all seem to rub along, and only once has someone gone to the wrong room and climbed into bed next to a stranger. Philippa was telling Kenny about it yesterday. It made her and Kaska laugh, and so did Kenny, in his now stilted and tilted fashion. I didn't, though I can see the funny side.

Now that Kenny's settled in, it should be less exhausting for Philippa. But, though she may no longer be nurse/carer/cleaner/cook, the worry of how he's being looked after in a strange place is a different, and no less tiring, duty.

To worry is a duty? That doesn't make sense. Does it?

She still occasionally talks about bringing Kenny home

when he's better, and the changes needed around the house to make it work. I know she wants to believe it can happen. I don't believe it can. I'm sorry.

The three of us are visiting today. In a manner I can't understand, I'm quite low today, despite a feeling of hope; perhaps because of the hope?

As predicted, Kenny's swallowing and speech deteriorate, but until such time as he can't swallow at all, we hold on to some hope. He cannot move his left arm and hand, but while he can move his right, we hold on to some hope. He doesn't entertain us with ditties anymore, but while he still smiles when Kaska sings the Sergeant Major or Knees Up songs, and holds hands when Philippa recites the Pussycat, Pussycat or Michaelmas Daisy rhyme, we hold on to some hope. He has good days and bad days. While he can look Philippa in the eye and say, however falteringly, 'I know you. I love you,' we hold on to much hope.

His love for us gives us hope.

Kaska has moved in to our house, pays rent and contributes to the bills, so she works as many hours as she can as a visiting carer, locally. I don't know how long she will stay. I don't mind. I'm not 'living' there full-time myself these days. I spend most nights with Kenny. So far they are treating him well and with respect, though perhaps not as much as he deserves, but then they won't know who he is; how he has lived. He was – is – a good man, whatever measure you care to use.

From Kenny's room we can see the big pond in the garden. The staff talk about taking Kenny out there in a wheelchair, when he's up for it and the weather is better. Philippa is holding Kenny's hand, quietly singing, 'Bye Bye Blackbird.' Kenny doesn't try to join in but he's smiling, until the chorus when he mumbles,

'Bevevie, why am … I …still here?' His speech is slurred but better than a week ago. So we have hope.

'It's me, Philippa, Dad.'

He's looking my way, not Philippa's, and I don't think he's confused. I believe he sees me; I know that's not true.

'Take me?' He makes it a question, as if his memory is as unsure as his now failing speech.

'Home?'

'With you, Bev.'

To Philippa, the words mean little, I hope. Or do I? Why wouldn't I hope she understands? For Kenny's sake, and perhaps mine, a little.

Philippa pecks him on the cheek. Her eyes are damp. 'I can't, Dad. I'm sorry.' She pulls his bed covers just an inch higher, desperate to pretend that perhaps there is a way of offering more comfort.

'Sorry,' whispers Kenny.

On the way home we stop off at the park. I haven't been here for so long. In the last few weeks I've got used to being out again. It was frightening at first but it's getting easier and when I feel a panic coming on I close my eyes and recite The Michaelmas Daisy. But today we've come back to *our* park, and I'm scared again. Philippa wants to show it to Kaska and it's a nice afternoon, but I'm worried it's not our park anymore. What if the shrubs and flower beds are gone? What if the playground area has been removed? What if the avenue of trees leading from the gate to the water fountain is no longer there? What if the water fountain is dry? I will be devastated. I am already so close to losing everything I cherish.

The park is ok(ish). It's not as well-tended as I remember and the playground apparatus is different; the witch's hat and the roundabout have gone. But there is enough there to keep a couple of young children happy as their mothers chat. The water fountain is there, but no one tries to use it so I can't say if it's still in use.

We take a bench on the path running round the park's edge. Philippa and Kaska sit close. They are comfortable with each other and don't need to fill silence. After a minute or two watching the children on the swings, Philippa asks, 'Do you know what Dad meant, when he asked to be taken?'

'To come home,' says Kaska.

Philippa is silent, and now I'm sure she knows what he meant, though it's too late for her to do anything. I hope she doesn't feel she has failed Kenny the way he and I failed each other. It's such a thing to ask. But, in a sense, asked she has been, and she loves him, and he loves her. Has he earned the right to ask? Either way, she's burdened.

'Perhaps not.' Philippa answers Kaska, taking the offered miniature Milky Way but not unwrapping it. 'But a woman's job is to give life, to protect it, isn't it?'

Kaska is confused, not following this train of thought, but she agrees, adding softly, 'Even if we don't all get the chance.'

'There is still time, for you,' says Philippa.

'If I meet the right person? Perhaps. Or I could adopt and be a single parent? So could you.'

'At my age? No, I nearly had my chance. It wasn't to be.'

'Nearly?'

Philippa looks down, and I think she's unsure about meeting Kaska's gaze. She mutters, 'I miscarried, twice. Long time ago.'

I am shocked and astonished. A bedlam of questions scramble through my thoughts. My stomach heaves and I am instantly devastated, but only for a moment, then I am angry. How dare Philippa not have told me? How dare she? I glare at her, to no purpose – of course I know that – then feel my own tears build as I look into her glistening eyes. She has shed more than enough for both of us, I've no doubt. Please God, give me a way to take the pain away from her.

Kaska is speechless, or, perhaps, knows there's nothing to be said. She awkwardly hugs Philippa.

'Ayden and Enda,' whispers Philippa. 'Ciaran wanted to give them Irish names. Ayden means little fire. Enda means little bird. Ciaran was distraught. I let him down.'

Kaska holds her tighter, 'That's not true.'

'It was a long time ago, before I turned forty. Afterwards we kept trying but nothing happened. And then I wanted to try IVF but Ciaran didn't, wouldn't. A few years passed and then it was too late. A few more years passed and every day was a reminder and then a resentment, of each other. We stopped laughing. We divorced.' Philippa forces a laugh, 'And him a Catholic.'

So now I know what happened to them. How could she not have told me? How could I not have told her about Sasha? Think how different it could have been if I had. Why did I think silence was protection, for either of us?

'What did your parents say?' Kaska asks.

'They never knew. I couldn't bear to hurt them. They would have been so disappointed, for me, not themselves, and so, so sad. For me. They worried so much. They loved so much. What hurt me was as bad for them. Worse.'

'You shouldn't feel guilty.'

'Too late,' says Philippa.

Watching over her has never been such agony as now. How was I so selfish? So foolish?

I was, am, a mother.

'Beautiful names, Ayden and ...' prompts Kaska.

'Enda.'

'Do you keep a vision of them?'

The drive home is in silence. Philippa ushers Kaska through the front door, upstairs and into her bedroom. I follow. The room is as neat and ordered as I expected. In the corner is the portrait, nearly finished. My breath is stolen. There are two toddlers. Two beautiful children, bursting with life and energy. One is a girl, with long dark hair and blue eyes. The other is a boy, taller than the girl, with a roundish face, and dark brown eyes. He has a small nose and pale mole on one cheek.

Philippa indicates to the girl, 'Ayden,' and the boy, 'Enda.'

Enda: a little bird.

Enda is a vision of my Sasha.

Kaska and Philippa are in the lounge, watching something on TV that has no interest for me. I'm in Kenny's empty bedroom. My guilt at not having told Philippa about Sasha, and the burden we placed on her with our suffocating worry through the years is deep and heavy. I can barely face her.

Philippa has Kaska for company.

I want to be with Kenny, I want to sit and hold his hand and cry while I tell him how I have failed. He will have a way of saying it's ok without ignoring or belittling my fear. He will have a way of making me feel I did the right thing, somehow.

I go to him.

The Michaelmas Daisy

Chapter 22
Friday 27th September
The Michaelmas Daisy

Philippa is in the garden, tidying. Deciding which plants should be left, trimmed, or culled. That was Kenny's job. I hated playing executioner. Though it's late September and the sun is low, it's warm and Philippa's a little flushed. Kaska calls to her through the open kitchen door, offering coffee. Philippa shouts back for a juice. As she walks back to the house she places the secateurs on the kneeling tray Kenny made for me so many years ago.

Kaska passes over Philippa's phone. 'It rang but I couldn't get there in time, sorry.'

Philippa checks the screen. 'It's Raymond. Your ex-roommate.' She feels the need to explain.

'Ah, that Raymond,' teases Kaska.

'He's coming to see Dad with us later. I'll give him a ring.'

Kaska laughs, 'Of course.'

Philippa flushes, gulps the juice and returns to the garden.

Kaska calls after her, 'Don't forget, Ruby's cutting your hair at two.'

This September day is bright enough for outdoor drying, and the smell of clean laundry comes to me: soapy; warm; damp; fresh. This would have been a good day to take Philippa to the library, or the shops to treat her to a Jamboree Bag, or just to show her off in a new coat, or perhaps to buy her first school uniform, or to the park. I miss the park. Of course, I miss being alive generally. But, more than anything, I miss being young. I miss doing new things for the first time. I miss anticipating those new experiences, ideas and people. As a young woman the possibilities were endless. It was ok to trust and be wrong sometimes. It was ok to catch a young man's eye – like Kenny's – smile openly, hold his gaze, believe he saw you as appealing, good looking, sexy even – not that sexy was a word we used back in the day – and saw you not only as you are and were, but, more importantly, who you could be – that was what it meant to be young. That's what I miss. I miss me and Kenny.

I would do it all again in a heartbeat.

Philippa stares at the purple Michaelmas daisies, perhaps a square yard of plants; a healthy, welcome display. The small flowers huddle together, the petals clustering bravely on top of spindly stems with small, spiky leaves. Individually they look fragile but, bunched as they are, maybe eighteen inches tall, they are bold and defiant, daring the autumn to come as they give the last of the summer colour. These Michaelmas daisies won't see over the garden wall, but they would have made Kenny smile, and he believed in them, I'm sure. Philippa is lost in thought, lost in reverie, I like to think, of late summer days with me and Kenny. Those days were full of promise, and it used to worry me that the promise might not have been fulfilled. These days I think it was the calm excitement of that promise that mattered, and being able to fleetingly grasp it again now is as important as any fulfilment. It keeps us believing in a future – and one worth believing in – which, of course, is ironic in my case. But I believe Philippa feels it too.

There is a future in nostalgia.

I hear the children from the nearby infants school shouting and laughing during their break. It was Philippa's first school. I used to come into the garden to listen, hoping to make out her voice.

A loud playground shriek – of excitement more than pain, I think – shakes Philippa's thoughts away and she phones Raymond. He seems a decent lad. Lad? He's two years younger than Philippa. So, yes, still a lad.

I have been flitting between Philippa's and the nursing home, but now it's time to choose. Kenny's waiting.

For the last eight years, watching over Philippa and Kenny has been my life, my vocation. I don't know if I've been good at it, but I think my epitaph would be simple: *She loved them truly, tried her best and gave her all.* But now I'm feeling it doesn't help Philippa to have me around, even though to not be part of her life is truly frightening; am I abandoning her? What will happen to her? How will she cope with Kenny's death? Will she find happiness? Might Raymond be an answer? Obvious questions, I know, but this is not the time to avoid simple truths.

So, it will be hard to leave her, but Kenny's need is greater. I don't blame Philippa for him being in Oak Meadows. I know she thinks about bringing him home, and not just because she feels guilty. She misses him terribly. She misses his smile, his love, his ditties. And, I'm sure, she misses being needed. But that's not true. Kenny still needs us. And we need him. He hardly talks now but his smile is enough to cheer us, and remind us of how our family lived and loved; how he provided for us, how he protected us, how we never doubted his devotion, how he made us laugh; a lifetime of memories in one simple smile.

Kenny's waiting.

I don't think I'll need to stay at the nursing home long. I hope not, for all our sakes. But wherever I am, I'll still be Philippa's mum. She knows me well enough that I am always with her; she is my daughter. I know her well enough that she is always with me; I am her mother.

Kenny's waiting. He can barely swallow and is sleeping for hours and hours. I wonder what will happen when he dies. I'm excited to find out – I have belief if not great faith – and feel that somewhere along the way we'll meet my Sasha and Philippa's Ayden and Enda. Who knows, maybe we'll all end up back here, watching over Philippa. That's a future worth believing in.

'Bye, Philippa, have a good day. Get what you can from it. It won't come round again.'

The Michaelmas daisy grows so tall
It sees right over the garden wall,
I wonder, I wonder what it can see
For the Michaelmas daisy is taller than me.

END

Author's Thanks

Although all the characters in this book are fictional, the story was inspired by Florence Kirby, and June and Raymond Marriner.

Florence is a wonderful carer who brought much hope, energy, love, skill and kindness to our family when it was most needed. Florence is also a gifted story teller, but I should stress this novel does not tell Florence's story; the character of Kaska in this novel is not based on Florence, other than they share the same gift of compassion and love of laughter. Florence's story is hers to tell and I hope she writes that story one day. We are blessed that she came into our lives.

Further inspiration came from other wonderful carers who we were fortunate enough to meet – Ali, Thomas, Dash, Joanna, Peter. All were dedicated professionals, but, just as important, they all had their own stories – each of which could be a novel in its own right.

If you are ever fortunate to meet (for whatever reason) a carer giving their all, then don't hesitate to ask after them; their own lives; their own stories. More likely than not you will be enthralled, and reminded of the breadth and depth of humanity.

No novel reaches the shelves without help and guidance, and without the people named below this book would still be languishing on a hard drive, forever tinkered with, but never finished. Thanks to them, I believed in it.

Editor, writing mentor and educator: Paul Swallow.

Beta readers: Kath Kyle, Angela Sherritt, Linda Laurie, Chris Troughton, Debbie Marriner

The Michaelmas Daisy

Thanks are also due to the Marriner and the Laurie families. When needed we came together, and found love and hope amongst us beyond that which we may have imagined – in large part due to our captain and compass, Linda.

And lastly, a deep and everlasting thank you to Raymond and June Marriner. Of all the many gifts they gave us, perhaps the greatest came at the last, bringing us close and helping us learn what it means to be human.

… by Paul Marriner and available through www.bluescalepublishing.co.uk .

Miracle Number Four

A song of the suburbs: a story of family, friends, first love, tragedy, hope and rock and roll

It's 1976 and with dreams of a career in rock, a crush on the prettiest girl in town, and a mother in remission from cancer, Mike's future looks bright.

Music brings excitement and a chance to shine, but life off-stage is complicated.

Together with family, friends and band-mates, Mike finds joy, sadness and loss. Troubling secrets surface while a new friend brings both fresh perspectives and a cruel reality. The radios and pubs blast rock into the suburban nights and the band prepare for their big break. Is Mike ready?

A warm, thoughtful, questioning novel; a reminder of simpler days, complicated emotions and music of a generation.

… by Paul Marriner and available through www.bluescalepublishing.co.uk .

Three Weeks In The Summer

Innocence Lost, Grief Found

1976. Richard (16) has finished his exams and a long, hot summer beckons, but his crush on the new girl in town is unrequited. He leaves the stifling suburb to spend time in The New Forest with Dudek, his Czech uncle. Dudek is being cared for by Anika, a vivacious young Czech woman. Anika introduces him to village life and when he meets Jennifer, a girl his age, he finds his attentions torn between them. Teenage emotions and needs are laid bare as relationships with the two girls develop.

The summer's experiences intensify as forest fires threaten the village and Richard learns more of the events that led to his father's death. As the summer break ends, Richard has been touched by love and death and understands more of his father's history.

The story concludes the following New Year when Richard returns to The New Forest, needing to pick up where the summer ended.

… by Paul Marriner and available through www.bluescalepublishing.co.uk .

The Tiger Curtain And Other Stories

Tigers, Wellington boots, angels, radios, old men, a China spaniel, young couples, shopping trolleys - all these and more in this eclectic collection of short stories and poems.

For the most part heart-warming, but occasionally sad and dark, these stories will provoke thought and emotion.

The collection includes The Radio - Lovereading People's Choice Short Story Winner 2021 (national award)

… by Paul Marriner and available through www.bluescalepublishing.co.uk .

The Blue Bench

A beautifully written story of yearning and love in 1920 as a nation grieves - one soul, one person at a time. The body of the Unknown Warrior is coming home, can Britain find peace?

'..an important novel..'

Margate 1920. The Great War is over but Britain mourns and its spirit is not yet mended.

Edward and William have returned from the front as changed men. Together they have survived grotesque horrors and remain haunted by memories of comrades who did not come home. The summer season in Margate is a chance for them to rebuild their lives and reconcile the past.

Evelyn and Catherine are young women ready to live life to the full. Their independence has been hard won and, with little knowledge of the cost of their freedom, they are ready to face new challenges side by side.

Can they define their own future and open their hearts to the prospect of finding love? Will the summer of 1920 be a turning point for these new friends? As the body of the Unknown Warrior is returned, can the nation find a way forward?

'..a brilliant story told brilliantly..'

... by Paul Marriner and available through www.bluescalepublishing.co.uk .

Sunrises

... moving and thought provoking ...

A story of a family learning how to love, lose, mourn and, ultimately, find peace.

When Anthony and Christine's daughter dies the void is unimaginable and unbearable. Grief is driving their family apart and they struggle to find peace. Mark, their son, is growing to manhood not sure of his place and seeking his own way forward.

Big questions have no answers and important truths hide hard lessons.

Love, grief, hope, sorrow and joy – bringing truth to a life.